WONDER TALES

The Book of Wonder
and
Tales of Wonder

WONDER TALES

The Book of Wonder
and
Tales of Wonder

LORD DUNSANY

DOVER PUBLICATIONS, INC.
Mineola, New York

Bibliographical Note

This Dover edition, first published in 2003, is an unabridged republication of two Lord Dunsany story collections bound together as one: *The Book of Wonder: A Chronicle of Little Adventures at the Edge of the World,* originally published in 1912 by John W. Luce & Company, Boston; and *Tales of Wonder,* originally published in 1916 by Elkin Mathews, London.

Library of Congress Cataloging-in-Publication Data

Dunsany, Edward John Moreton Drax Plunkett, Baron, 1878–1957.
   [Book of wonder]
   Wonder tales / Lord Dunsany.
      p. cm.
   Contents: The book of wonder — Tales of wonder.
   ISBN 0-486-43201-7 (pbk.)
      1. Fantasy fiction, English. I. Dunsany, Edward John Moreton Drax Plunkett, Baron, 1878–1957. Tales of wonder. II. Title.

PR6007.U6B6 2003
823'.912—dc21   2003048971

Manufactured in the United States of America
Dover Publications, Inc., 31 East 2nd Street, Mineola, N.Y. 11501

Contents

The Book of Wonder

PAGE

The Bride of the Man-Horse   1
Distressing Tale of Thangobrind the Jeweller   5
The House of the Sphinx   9
Probable Adventure of the Three Literary Men   12
The Injudicious Prayers of Pombo the Idolater   16
The Loot of Bombasharna   20
Miss Cubbidge and the Dragon of Romance   24
The Quest of the Queen's Tears   27
The Hoard of the Gibbelins   32
How Nuth Would Have Practised His Art Upon the Gnoles   36
How One Came, as Was Foretold, to the City of Never   41
The Coronation of Mr. Thomas Shap   45
Chu-bu and Sheemish   49
The Wonderful Window   53
Epilogue   58

Tales of Wonder

PAGE

A Tale of London   61
Thirteen at Table   64
The City on Mallington Moor   72
Why the Milkman Shudders When He Perceives the Dawn   79
The Bad Old Woman in Black   82
The Bird of the Difficult Eye   84

The Long Porter's Tale   88
The Bureau d'Echange de Maux   93
A Story of Land and Sea   97
The Loot of Loma   118
A Tale of the Equator   122
A Narrow Escape   125
The Watch-Tower   127
The Secret of the Sea   130
How Plash-Goo Came to the Land of None's Desire   134
The Three Sailors' Gambit   136
How Ali Came to the Black Country   144
The Exiles' Club   148
The Three Infernal Jokes   153

The Book of Wonder

Preface

COME with me, ladies and gentlemen
who are in any wise weary of London:
come with me: and those that tire at all
of the world we know: for we have new
worlds here.

The Bride of the Man-Horse

In the morning of his two hundred and fiftieth year Shepperalk the centaur went to the golden coffer, wherein the treasure of the centaurs was, and taking from it the hoarded amulet that his father, Jyshak, in the years of his prime, had hammered from mountain gold and set with opals bartered from the gnomes, he put it upon his wrist, and said no word, but walked from his mother's cavern. And he took with him too that clarion of the centaurs, that famous silver horn, that in its time had summoned to surrender seventeen cities of Man, and for twenty years had brayed at star-girt walls in the Siege of Tholdenblarna, the citadel of the gods, what time the centaurs waged their fabulous war and were not broken by any force of arms, but retreated slowly in a cloud of dust before the final miracle of the gods that They brought in Their desperate need from Their ultimate armoury. He took it and strode away, and his mother only sighed and let him go.

She knew that to-day he would not drink at the stream coming down from the terraces of Varpa Niger, the inner land of the mountains, that to-day he would not wonder awhile at the sunset and afterwards trot back to the cavern again to sleep on rushes pulled by rivers that know not Man. She knew that it was with him as it had been of old with his father, and with Goom the father of Jyshak, and long ago with the gods. Therefore she only sighed and let him go.

But he, coming out from the cavern that was his home, went for the first time over the little stream, and going round the corner of the crags saw glittering beneath him the mundane plain. And the wind of the autumn that was gilding the world, rushing up the slopes of the mountain, beat cold on his naked flanks. He raised his head and snorted.

"I am a man-horse now!" he shouted aloud; and leaping from crag to crag he galloped by valley and chasm, by torrent-bed and scar of avalanche, until he came to the wandering leagues of the plain, and left behind him for ever the Athraminaurian mountains.

1

His goal was Zretazoola, the city of Sombelenë. What legend
of Sombelenë's inhuman beauty or of the wonder of her mystery had ever floated over the mundane plain to the fabulous
cradle of the centaurs' race, the Athraminaurian mountains, I
do not know. Yet in the blood of man there is a tide, an old sea-
current, rather, that is somehow akin to the twilight, which
brings him rumours of beauty from however far away, as drift-
wood is found at sea from islands not yet discovered; and this
spring-tide or current that visits the blood of man comes from
the fabulous quarter of his lineage, from the legendary, of old;
it takes him out to the woodlands, out to the hills; he listens to
ancient song. So it may be that Shepperalk's fabulous blood
stirred in those lonely mountains away at the edge of the world
to rumours that only the airy twilight knew and only confided
secretly to the bat, for Shepperalk was more legendary even
than man. Certain it was that he headed from the first for the
city Zretazoola, where Sombelenë in her temple dwelt; though
all the mundane plain, its rivers and mountains, lay between
Shepperalk's home and the city he sought.

When first the feet of the centaur touched the grass of that soft
alluvial earth he blew for joy upon the silver horn, he pranced and
caracoled, he gambolled over the leagues; pace came to him like a
maiden with a lamp, a new and beautiful wonder; the wind
laughed as it passed him. He put his head down low to the scent
of the flowers, he lifted it up to be nearer the unseen stars, he rev-
elled through kingdoms, took rivers in his stride; how shall I tell
you, ye that dwell in cities, how shall I tell you what he felt as he
galloped? He felt for strength like the towers of Bel-Narāna; for
lightness like those gossamer palaces that the fairy-spider builds
'twixt heaven and sea along the coasts of Zith; for swiftness like
some bird racing up from the morning to sing in some city's spires
before daylight comes. He was the sworn companion of the wind.
For joy he was as a song; the lightnings of his legendary sires, the
earlier gods, began to mix with his blood; his hooves thundered.
He came to the cities of men, and all men trembled, for they
remembered the ancient mythical wars, and now they dreaded
new battles and feared for the race of man. Not by Clio are these
wars recorded, history does not know them, but what of that? Not
all of us have sat at historians' feet, but all have learned fable and
myth at their mothers' knees. And there were none that did not
fear strange wars when they saw Shepperalk swerve and leap
along the public ways. So he passed from city to city.

By night he lay down unpanting in the reeds of some marsh or forest; before dawn he rose triumphant, and hugely drank of some river in the dark, and splashing out of it would trot to some high place to find the sunrise, and to send echoing eastwards the exultant greetings of his jubilant horn. And lo! the sunrise coming up from the echoes, and the plains new-lit by the day, and the leagues spinning by like water flung from a top, and that gay companion, the loudly laughing wind, and men and the fears of men and their little cities; and, after that, great rivers and waste spaces and huge new hills, and then new lands beyond them, and more cities of men, and always the old companion, the glorious wind. Kingdom by kingdom slipt by, and still his breath was even. "It is a golden thing to gallop on good turf in one's youth," said the young man-horse, the centaur. "Ha, ha," said the wind of the hills, and the winds of the plain answered.

Bells pealed in frantic towers, wise men consulted parchments, astrologers sought of the portent from the stars, the aged made subtle prophecies. "Is he not swift?" said the young. "How glad he is," said the children.

Night after night brought him sleep, and day after day lit his gallop, till he came to the lands of the Athalonian men who live by the edges of the mundane plain, and from them he came to the lands of legend again such as those in which he was cradled on the other side of the world, and which fringe the marge of the world and mix with the twilight. And there a mighty thought came into his untired heart, for he knew that he neared Zretazoola now, the city of Sombelenë.

It was late in the day when he neared it, and clouds coloured with evening rolled low on the plain before him; he galloped on into their golden mist, and when it hid from his eyes the sight of things, the dreams in his heart awoke and romantically he pondered all those rumours that used to come to him from Sombelenë, because of the fellowship of fabulous things. She dwelt (said evening secretly to the bat) in a little temple by a lone lake-shore. A grove of cypresses screened her from the city, from Zretazoola of the climbing ways. And opposite her temple stood her tomb, her sad lake-sepulchre with open door, lest her amazing beauty and the centuries of her youth should ever give rise to the heresy among men that lovely Sombelenë was immortal: for only her beauty and her lineage were divine.

Her father had been half centaur and half god; her mother

was the child of a desert lion and that sphinx that watches the
pyramids;—she was more mystical than Woman.

Her beauty was as a dream, was as a song; the one dream of a
lifetime dreamed on enchanted dews, the one song sung to some
city by a deathless bird blown far from his native coasts by storm
in Paradise. Dawn after dawn on mountains of romance or twilight after twilight could never equal her beauty; all the glow-
worms had not the secret among them nor all the stars of night;
poets had never sung it nor evening guessed its meaning; the
morning envied it, it was hidden from lovers.

She was unwed, unwooed.

The lions came not to woo her because they feared her strength,
and the gods dared not love her because they knew she must die.

This was what evening had whispered to the bat, this was the
dream in the heart of Shepperalk as he cantered blind through
the mist. And suddenly there at his hooves in the dark of the
plain appeared the cleft in the legendary lands, and Zretazoola
sheltering in the cleft, and sunning herself in the evening.

Swiftly and craftily he bounded down by the upper end of the
cleft, and entering Zretazoola by the outer gate which looks out
sheer on the stars, he galloped suddenly down the narrow
streets. Many that rushed out on to balconies as he went clattering by, many that put their heads from glittering windows,
are told of in olden song. Shepperalk did not tarry to give
greetings or to answer challenges from martial towers, he was
down through the earthward gateway like the thunderbolt of
his sires, and, like Leviathan who has leapt at an eagle, he
surged into the water between temple and tomb.

He galloped with half-shut eyes up the temple-steps, and,
only seeing dimly through his lashes, seized Sombelenë by the
hair, undazzled as yet by her beauty, and so haled her away;
and, leaping with her over the floorless chasm where the
waters of the lake fall unremembered away into a hole in the
world, took her we know not where, to be her slave for all those
centuries that are allowed to his race.

Three blasts he gave as he went upon that silver horn that
is the world-old treasure of the centaurs. These were his
wedding bells.

Distressing Tale of Thangobrind the Jeweller

When Thangobrind the jeweller heard the ominous cough, he turned at once upon that narrow way. A thief was he, of very high repute, being patronised by the lofty and elect, for he stole nothing smaller than the Moomoo's egg, and in all his life stole only four kinds of stone—the ruby, the diamond, the emerald, and the sapphire; and, as jewellers go, his honesty was great. Now there was a Merchant Prince who had come to Thangobrind and had offered his daughter's soul for the diamond that is larger than the human head and was to be found on the lap of the spider-idol, Hlo-hlo, in his temple of Moung-ga-ling; for he had heard that Thangobrind was a thief to be trusted.

Thangobrind oiled his body and slipped out of his shop, and went secretly through byways, and got as far as Snarp, before anybody knew that he was out on business again or missed his sword from its place under the counter. Thence he moved only by night, hiding by day and rubbing the edges of his sword, which he called Mouse because it was swift and nimble. The jeweller had subtle methods of travelling; nobody saw him cross the plains of Zid; nobody saw him come to Mursk or Tlun. O, but he loved shadows! Once the moon peeping out unexpectedly from a tempest had betrayed an ordinary jeweller; not so did it undo Thangobrind: the watchman only saw a crouching shape that snarled and laughed: "'Tis but a hyena," they said. Once in the city of Ag one of the guardians seized him, but Thangobrind was oiled and slipped from his hand; you scarcely heard his bare feet patter away. He knew that the Merchant Prince awaited his return, his little eyes open all night and glittering with greed; he knew how his daughter lay chained up and screaming night and day. Ah, Thangobrind knew. And had he not been out on business he had almost allowed himself one or two little laughs. But business was business, and the diamond that he sought still lay on the lap of Hlo-hlo, where it had been for the last two million years since Hlo-hlo created the world and gave unto it all things except that precious stone called Dead Man's Diamond. The jewel was often stolen, but it had a knack of coming back again to the lap of Hlo-hlo. Thangobrind knew this, but he was no common jeweller and hoped to outwit Hlo-hlo, perceiving not the trend of ambition and lust and that they are vanity.

How nimbly he threaded his way through the pits of Snood!— now like a botanist, scrutinising the ground; now like a dancer, leaping from crumbling edges. It was quite dark when he went by the towers of Tor, where archers shoot ivory arrows at strangers lest any foreigner should alter their laws, which are bad, but not to be altered by mere aliens. At night they shoot by the sound of the strangers' feet. O, Thangobrind, Thangobrind, was ever a jeweller like you! He dragged two stones behind him by long cords, and at these the archers shot. Tempting indeed was the snare that they set in Woth, the emeralds loose-set in the city's gate; but Thangobrind discerned the golden cord that climbed the wall from each and the weights that would topple upon him if he touched one, and so he left them, though he left them weeping, and at last came to Theth. There all men worship Hlo-hlo; though they are willing to believe in other gods, as missionaries attest, but only as creatures of the chase for the hunting of Hlo-hlo, who wears Their halos, so these people say, on golden hooks along his hunting-belt. And from Theth he came to the city of Moung and the temple of Moung-ga-ling, and entered and saw the spider-idol, Hlo-hlo, sitting there with Dead Man's Diamond glittering on his lap, and looking for all the world like a full moon, but a full moon seen by a lunatic who had slept too long in its rays, for there was in Dead Man's Diamond a certain sinister look and a boding of things to happen that are better not mentioned here. The face of the spider-idol was lit by that fatal gem; there was no other light. In spite of his shocking limbs and that demoniac body, his face was serene and apparently unconscious.

A little fear came into the mind of Thangobrind the jeweller, a passing tremor—no more; business was business and he hoped for the best. Thangobrind offered honey to Hlo-hlo and prostrated himself before him. Oh, he was cunning! When the priests stole out of the darkness to lap up the honey they were stretched senseless on the temple floor, for there was a drug in the honey that was offered to Hlo-hlo. And Thangobrind the jeweller picked Dead Man's Diamond up and put it on his shoulder and trudged away from the shrine; and Hlo-hlo the spider-idol said nothing at all, but he laughed softly as the jeweller shut the door. When the priests awoke out of the grip of the drug that was offered with the honey to Hlo-hlo, they rushed to a little secret room with an outlet on the stars and cast a horoscope of the thief. Something that they saw in the horoscope seemed to satisfy the priests.

It was not like Thangobrind to go back up the road by which he had come. No, he went by another road, even though it led to the narrow way, night-house and spider-forest.

The city of Moung went towering up behind him, balcony above balcony, eclipsing half the stars, as he trudged away with his diamond. He was not easy as he trudged away. Though when a soft pittering as of velvet feet arose behind him he refused to acknowledge that it might be what he feared, yet the instincts of his trade told him that it is not well when any noise whatever follows a diamond by night, and this was one of the largest that had ever come to him in the way of business. When he came to the narrow way that leads to spider-forest, Dead Man's Diamond feeling cold and heavy, and the velvety footfall seeming fearfully close, the jeweller stopped and almost hesitated. He looked behind him; there was nothing there. He listened attentively; there was no sound now. Then he thought of the screams of the Merchant Prince's daughter, whose soul was the diamond's price, and smiled and went stoutly on. There watched him, apathetically, over the narrow way, that grim and dubious woman whose house is Night. Thangobrind, hearing no longer the sound of suspicious feet, felt easier now. He was all but come to the end of the narrow way, when the woman listlessly uttered that ominous cough.

The cough was too full of meaning to be disregarded. Thangobrind turned round and saw at once what he feared. The spider-idol had not stayed at home. The jeweller put his diamond gently upon the ground and drew his sword called Mouse. And then began that famous fight upon the narrow way in which the grim old woman whose house was Night seemed to take so little interest. To the spider-idol you saw at once it was all a horrible joke. To the jeweller it was grim earnest. He fought and panted and was pushed back slowly along the narrow way, but he wounded Hlo-hlo all the while with terrible long gashes all over his deep, soft body till Mouse

8   THE BOOK OF WONDER

was slimy with blood. But at last the persistent laughter of Hlo-hlo was too much for the jeweller's nerves, and, once more wounding his demoniac foe, he sank aghast and exhausted by the door of the house called Night at the feet of the grim old woman, who having uttered once that ominous cough interfered no further with the course of events. And there carried Thangobrind the jeweller away those whose duty it was, to the house where the two men hang, and taking down from his hook the left-hand one of the two, they put that venturous jeweller in his place; so that there fell on him the doom that he feared, as all men know though it is so long since, and there abated somewhat the ire of the envious gods.

And the only daughter of the Merchant Prince felt so little gratitude for this great deliverance that she took to respectability of the militant kind, and became aggressively dull, and called her home the English Riviera, and had platitudes worked in worsted upon her tea-cosy, and in the end never died, but passed away in her residence.

The House of the Sphinx

When I came to the House of the Sphinx it was already dark. They made me eagerly welcome. And I, in spite of the deed, was glad of any shelter from that ominous wood. I saw at once that there had been a deed, although a cloak did all that a cloak may do to conceal it. The mere uneasiness of the welcome made me suspect that cloak.

The Sphinx was moody and silent. I had not come to pry into the secrets of Eternity nor to investigate the Sphinx's private life, and so had little to say and few questions to ask; but to whatever I did say she remained morosely indifferent. It was clear that either she suspected me of being in search of the secrets of one of her gods, or of being boldly inquisitive about her traffic with Time, or else she was darkly absorbed with brooding upon the deed.

I saw soon enough that there was another than me to welcome; I saw it from the hurried way that they glanced from the door to the deed and back to the door again. And it was clear that the welcome was to be a bolted door. But such bolts, and such a door! Rust and decay and fungus had been there far too long, and it was not a barrier any longer that would keep out even a determined wolf. And it seemed to be something worse than a wolf that they feared.

A little later on I gathered from what they said that some imperious and ghastly thing was looking for the Sphinx, and that something that had happened had made its arrival certain. It appeared that they had slapped the Sphinx to vex her out of her apathy in order that she should pray to one of her gods, whom she had littered in the house of Time; but her moody silence was invincible, and her apathy Oriental, ever since the deed had happened. And when they found that they could not make her pray, there was nothing for them to do but to pay little useless attentions to the rusty lock of the door, and to look at the deed and wonder, and even pretend to hope, and to say that after all it might not bring that destined thing from the forest, which no one named.

9

It may be said I had chosen a gruesome house, but not if I had described the forest from which I came, and I was in need of any spot wherein I could rest my mind from the thought of it.

I wondered very much what thing would come from the forest on account of the deed; and having seen that forest—as you, gentle reader, have not—I had the advantage of knowing that anything might come. It was useless to ask the Sphinx— she seldom reveals things, like her paramour Time (the gods take after her), and while this mood was on her, rebuff was certain. So I quietly began to oil the lock of the door. And as soon as they saw this simple act I won their confidence. It was not that my work was of any use—it should have been done long before; but they saw that my interest was given for the moment to the thing that they thought vital. They clustered round me then. They asked me what I thought of the door, and whether I had seen better, and whether I had seen worse; and I told them about all the doors I knew, and said that the doors of the baptistery in Florence were better doors, and the doors made by a certain firm of builders in London were worse. And then I asked them what it was that was coming after the Sphinx because of the deed. And at first they would not say, and I stopped oiling the door; and then they said that it was the arch-inquisitor of the forest, who is investigator and avenger of all silverstrian things; and from all that they said about him it seemed to me that this person was quite white, and was a kind of madness that would settle down quite blankly upon a place, a kind of mist in which reason could not live; and it was the fear of this that made them fumble nervously at the lock of that rotten door; but with the Sphinx it was not so much fear as sheer prophecy.

The hope that they tried to hope was well enough in its way, but I did not share it; it was clear that the thing that they feared was the corollary of the deed—one saw that more by the resignation upon the face of the Sphinx than by their sorry anxiety for the door.

The wind soughed, and the great tapers flared, and their obvious fear and the silence of the Sphinx grew more than ever a part of the atmosphere, and bats went restlessly through the gloom of the wind that beat the tapers low.

Then a few things screamed far off, then a little nearer, and something was coming towards us, laughing hideously. I hastily gave a prod to the door that they guarded; my finger sank right into the mouldering wood—there was not a chance of holding it. I had not leisure to observe their fright; I thought of the back-door, for the forest was better than this; only the Sphinx was absolutely calm, her prophecy was made and she seemed to have seen her doom, so that no new thing could perturb her.

But by mouldering rungs of ladders as old as Man, by slippery edges of the dreaded abyss, with an ominous dizziness about my heart and a feeling of horror in the soles of my feet, I clambered from tower to tower till I found the door that I sought; and it opened on to one of the upper branches of a huge and sombre pine, down which I climbed on to the floor of the forest. And I was glad to be back again in the forest from which I had fled.

And the Sphinx in her menaced house—I know not how she fared—whether she gazes for ever, disconsolate, at the deed, remembering only in her smitten mind, at which the little boys now leer, that she once knew well those things at which man stands aghast; or whether in the end she crept away, and clambering horribly from abyss to abyss, came at last to higher things, and is wise and eternal still. For who knows of madness whether it is divine or whether it be of the pit?

Probable Adventure of the Three Literary Men

When the nomads came to El Lola they had no more songs, and the question of stealing the golden box arose in all its magnitude. On the one hand, many had sought the golden box, the receptacle (as the Aethiopians know) of poems of fabulous value; and their doom is still the common talk of Arabia. On the other hand, it was lonely to sit round the camp-fire by night with no new songs.

It was the tribe of Heth that discussed these things one evening upon the plains below the peak of Mluna. Their native land was the track across the world of immemorial wanderers; and there was trouble among the elders of the nomads because there were no new songs; while, untouched by human trouble, untouched as yet by the night that was hiding the plains away, the peak of Mluna, calm in the after-glow, looked on the Dubious Land. And it was there on the plain upon the known side of Mluna, just as the evening star came mouse-like into view and the flames of the camp-fire lifted their lonely plumes uncheered by any song that that rash scheme was hastily planned by the nomads which the world has named The Quest of the Golden Box.

No measure of wiser precaution could the elders of the nomads have taken than to choose for their thief that very Slith, that identical thief that (even as I write) in how many school-rooms governesses teach stole a march on the King of Westalia. Yet the weight of the box was such that others had to accompany him, and Sippy and Slorg were no more agile thieves than may be found to-day among vendors of the antique.

So over the shoulder of Mluna these three climbed next day and slept as well as they might among its snows rather than risk a night in the woods of the Dubious Land. And the morning came up radiant and the birds were full of song, but the forest underneath and the waste beyond it and the bare and ominous crags all wore the appearance of an unuttered threat.

12

Though Slith had an experience of twenty years of theft, yet he said little; only if one of the others made a stone roll with his foot, or, later on in the forest, if one of them stepped on a twig, he whispered sharply to them always the same words: "That is not business." He knew that he could not make them better thieves during a two-days' journey, and whatever doubts he had he interfered no further.

From the shoulder of Mluna they dropped into the clouds, and from the clouds to the forest, to whose native beasts, as well the three thieves knew, all flesh was meat, whether it were the flesh of fish or man. There the thieves drew idolatrously from their pockets each one a separate god and prayed for protection in the unfortunate wood, and hoped therefrom for a threefold chance of escape, since if anything should eat one of them it were certain to eat them all, and they confided that the corollary might be true and all should escape if one did. Whether one of these gods was propitious and awake, or whether all of the three, or whether it was chance that brought them through the forest unmouthed by detestable beasts, none knoweth; but certainly neither the emissaries of the god that most they feared, nor the wrath of the topical god of that ominous place, brought their doom to the three adventurers there or then. And so it was that they came to Rumbly Heath, in the heart of the Dubious Land, whose stormy hillocks were the ground-swell and the after-wash of the earthquake lulled for a while. Something so huge that it seemed unfair to man that it should move so softly stalked splendidly by them, and only so barely did they escape its notice that one word ran and echoed through their three imaginations—"If—if—if." And when this danger was at last gone by they moved cautiously on again and presently saw the little harmless mipt, half fairy and half gnome, giving shrill, contented squeaks on the edge of the world. And they edged away unseen, for they said that the inquisitiveness of the mipt had become fabulous, and that, harmless as he was, he had a bad way with secrets; yet they probably loathed the way that he nuzzles dead white bones, and would not admit their loathing, for it does not become adventurers to care who eats their bones. Be this as it may, they edged away from the mipt, and came almost at once to the wizened tree, the goal-post of their adventure, and knew that beside them was the crack in the world and the bridge from Bad to Worse, and that underneath them stood the rocky house of the Owner of the Box.

This was their simple plan: to slip into the corridor in the upper cliff; to run softly down it (of course with naked feet) under the warning to travellers that is graven upon stone, which interpreters take to be "It Is Better Not"; not to touch the berries that are there for a purpose, on the right side going down; and so to come to the guardian on his pedestal who had slept for a thousand years and should be sleeping still; and go in through the open window. One man was to wait outside by the crack in the World until the others came out with the golden box, and, should they cry for help, he was to threaten at once to unfasten the iron clamp that kept the crack together. When the box was secured they were to travel all night and all the following day, until the cloud-banks that wrapped the slopes of Mluna were well between them and the Owner of the Box.

The door in the cliff was open. They passed without a murmur down the cold steps, Slith leading them all the way. A glance of longing, no more, each gave to the beautiful berries. The guardian upon his pedestal was still asleep. Slorg climbed by a ladder, that Slith knew where to find, to the iron clamp across the crack in the World, and waited beside it with a chisel in his hand, listening closely for anything untoward, while his friends slipped into the house; and no sound came. And presently Slith and Sippy found the golden box: everything seemed happening as they had planned, it only remained to see if it was the right one and to escape with it from that dreadful place. Under the shelter of the pedestal, so near to the guardian that they could feel his warmth, which paradoxically had the effect of chilling the blood of the boldest of them, they smashed the emerald hasp and opened the golden box; and there they read by the light of ingenious sparks which Slith knew how to contrive, and even this poor light they hid with their bodies. What was their joy, even at that perilous moment, as they lurked between the guardian and the abyss, to find that the box contained fifteen peerless odes in the alcaic form, five sonnets that were by far the most beautiful in the world, nine ballads in the manner of Provence that had no equal in the treasuries of man, a poem addressed to a moth in twenty-eight perfect stanzas, a piece of blank verse of over a hundred lines on a level not yet known to have been attained by man, as well as fifteen lyrics on which no merchant would dare to set a price. They would have read them again, for they gave happy tears to a man and memories of dear things done in infancy, and brought sweet voices from far sepulchres; but Slith pointed imperiously to the way by which they had come, and extinguished the light; and Slorg and Sippy sighed, then took the box.

The guardian still slept the sleep that survived a thousand years.

As they came away they saw that indulgent chair close by the edge of the World in which the Owner of the Box had lately sat reading selfishly and alone the most beautiful songs and verses that poet ever dreamed.

They came in silence to the foot of the stairs; and then it befell that as they drew nearer safety, in the night's most secret hour, some hand in an upper chamber lit a shocking light, lit it and made no sound.

For a moment it might have been an ordinary light, fatal as even that could very well be at such a moment as this; but when it began to follow them like an eye and to grow redder and redder as it watched them, then even optimism despaired.

And Sippy very unwisely attempted flight, and Slorg even as unwisely tried to hide; but Slith, knowing well why that light was lit in that secret chamber and *who* it was that lit it, leaped over the edge of the World and is falling from us still through the unreverberate blackness of the abyss.

The Injudicious Prayers of Pombo the Idolater

Pombo the idolater had prayed to Ammuz a simple prayer, a necessary prayer, such as even an idol of ivory could very easily grant, and Ammuz has not immediately granted it. Pombo had therefore prayed to Tharma for the overthrow of Ammuz, an idol friendly to Tharma, and in doing this offended against the etiquette of the gods. Tharma refused to grant the little prayer. Pombo prayed frantically to all the gods of idolatry, for though it was a simple matter, yet it was very necessary to a man. And gods that were older than Ammuz rejected the prayers of Pombo, and even gods that were younger and therefore of greater repute. He prayed to them one by one, and they all refused to hear him; nor at first did he think at all of the subtle, divine etiquette against which he had offended. It occurred to him all at once as he prayed to his fiftieth idol, a little green-jade god whom the Chinese know, that all the idols were in league against him. When Pombo discovered this he resented his birth bitterly, and made lamentation and alleged that he was lost. He might have been seen then in any part of London haunting curiosity-shops and places where they sold idols of ivory or of stone, for he dwelt in London with others of his race though he was born in Burmah among those who hold Ganges holy. On drizzly evenings of November's worst his haggard face could be seen in the glow of some shop pressed close against the glass, where he would supplicate some calm cross-legged idol till policemen moved him on. And after closing hours back he would go to his dingy room, in that part of our capital where English is seldom spoken, to supplicate little idols of his own. And when Pombo's simple, necessary prayer was equally refused by the idols of museums, auction-rooms, shops, then he took counsel with himself and purchased incense and burned it in a brazier before his own cheap little idols, and played the while upon an instrument such as that wherewith men charm snakes. And still the idols clung to their etiquette.

16

Whether Pombo knew about this etiquette and considered it frivolous in the face of his need, or whether his need, now grown desperate, unhinged his mind, I know not, but Pombo the idolater took a stick and suddenly turned iconoclast.

Pombo the iconoclast immediately left his house, leaving his idols to be swept away with the dust and so to mingle with Man, and went to an arch-idolater of repute who carved idols out of rare stones, and put his case before him. The arch-idolater who made idols of his own rebuked Pombo in the name of Man for having broken his idols—"for hath not Man made them?" the arch-idolater said; and concerning the idols themselves he spoke long and learnedly, explaining divine etiquette, and how Pombo had offended, and how no idol in the world would listen to Pombo's prayer. When Pombo heard this he wept and made bitter outcry, and cursed the gods of ivory and the gods of jade, and the hand of Man that made them, but most of all he cursed their etiquette that had undone, as he said, an innocent man; so that at last that arch-idolater, who made idols of his own, stopped in his work upon an idol of jasper for a king that was weary of Wōsh, and took compassion on Pombo, and told him that though no idol in the world would listen to his prayer, yet only a little way over the edge of it a certain disreputable idol sat who knew nothing of etiquette, and granted prayers that no respectable god would ever consent to hear. When Pombo heard this he took two handfuls of the arch-idolater's beard and kissed them joyfully, and dried his tears and became his old impertinent self again. And he that carved from jasper the usurper of Wōsh explained how in the village of World's End, at the furthest end of Last Street, there is a hole that you take to be a well, close by the garden wall, but that if you lower yourself by your hands over the edge of the hole, and feel about with your feet till they find a ledge, that is the top step of a flight of stairs that takes you down over the edge of the World. "For all that men know, those stairs may have a purpose and even a bottom step," said the arch-idolater, "but discussion about the lower flights is idle." Then the teeth of Pombo chattered, for he feared the darkness, but he that made idols of his own explained that those stairs were always lit by the faint blue gloaming in which the World spins. "Then," he said, "you will go by Lonely House and under the bridge that leads from the House to Nowhere, and whose purpose is not guessed; thence past Maharrion, the god of flowers, and his high-priest, who is neither bird nor cat; and so you will come to the little idol Duth, the disreputable god that will grant your prayer." And he went on carving again at his idol of jasper for the king who was weary of Wōsh; and Pombo thanked him and went singing away, for in his vernacular mind he thought that "he *had* the gods."

It is a long journey from London to World's End, and Pombo had no money left, yet within five weeks he was strolling along Last Street; but how he contrived to get there I will not say, for it was not entirely honest. And Pombo found the well at the end of the garden beyond the end house of Last Street, and many thoughts ran through his mind as he hung by his hands from the edge, but chiefest of all those thoughts was one that said the gods were laughing at him through the mouth of the arch-idolater, their prophet, and the thought beat in his head till it ached like his wrists . . . and then he found the step.

And Pombo walked downstairs. There, sure enough, was the gloaming in which the world spins, and stars shone far off in it faintly; there was nothing before him as he went downstairs but that strange blue waste of gloaming, with its multitude of stars, and comets plunging through it on outward journeys and comets returning home. And then he saw the lights of the bridge to Nowhere, and all of a sudden he was in the glare of the shimmering parlour-window of Lonely House; and he heard voices there pronouncing words, and the voices were nowise human, and but for his bitter need he had screamed and fled. Halfway between the voices and Maharrion, whom he now saw standing out from the world, covered in rainbow halos, he perceived the weird grey beast that is neither cat nor bird. As Pombo hesitated, chilly with fear, he heard those voices grow louder in Lonely House, and at that he stealthily moved a few steps lower, and then rushed past the beast. The beast intently watched Maharrion hurling up bubbles that are every one a season of spring in unknown constellations, calling the swallows home to unimagined fields, watched him without even turning to look at Pombo, and saw him drop into the Linlunlarna, the river that rises at the edge of the World, the golden pollen that sweetens the tide of the river and is carried away from the World to be a joy to the Stars. And there before Pombo was the little disreputable god who cares nothing for etiquette and will answer prayers that are refused by all the respectable idols. And whether the view of him, at last, excited

Pombo's eagerness, or whether his need was greater than he could bear that it drove him so swiftly downstairs, or whether, as is most likely, he ran too fast past the beast, I do not know, and it does not matter to Pombo; but at any rate he could not stop, as he had designed, in attitude of prayer at the feet of Duth, but ran on past him down the narrowing steps, clutching at smooth bare rocks till he fell from the World as, when our hearts miss a beat, we fall in dreams and wake up with a dreadful jolt; but there was no waking up for Pombo, who still fell on towards the incurious stars, and his fate is even one with the fate of Slith.

The Loot of Bombasharna

Things had grown too hot for Shard, captain of pirates, on all the seas that he knew. The ports of Spain were closed to him; they knew him in San Domingo; men winked in Syracuse when he went by; the two Kings of the Sicilies never smiled within an hour of speaking of him; there were huge rewards for his head in every capital city, with pictures of it for identification—*and all the pictures were unflattering.* Therefore Captain Shard decided that the time had come to tell his men the secret.

Riding off Teneriffe one night, he called them all together. He generously admitted that there were things in the past that might require explanation: the crowns that the Princes of Aragon had sent to their nephews the Kings of the two Americas had certainly never reached their Most Sacred Majesties. Where, men might ask, were the eyes of Captain Stobbud? Who had been burning towns on the Patagonian seaboard? Why should such a ship as theirs choose pearls for cargo? Why so much blood on the decks and so many guns? And where was the *Nancy,* the *Lark,* or the *Margaret Belle*? Such questions as these, he urged, might be asked by the inquisitive, and if counsel for the defence should happen to be a fool, and unacquainted with the ways of the sea, they might become involved in troublesome legal formulae. And Bloody Bill, as they rudely called Mr. Gagg, a member of the crew, looked up at the sky, and said that it was a windy night and looked like hanging. And some of those present thoughtfully stroked their necks while Captain Shard unfolded to them his plan. He said the time was come to quit the *Desperate Lark,* for she was too well known to the navies of four kingdoms, and a fifth was getting to know her, and others had suspicions. (More cutters than even Captain Shard suspected were already looking for her jolly black flag with its neat skull-and-crossbones in yellow.) There was a little archipelago that he knew of on the wrong side of the Sargasso Sea; there were about thirty islands

20

there, bare, ordinary islands, but one of them floated. He had noticed it years ago, and had gone ashore and never told a soul, but had quietly anchored it with the anchor of his ship to the bottom of the sea, which just there was profoundly deep, and had made the thing the secret of his life, determining to marry and settle down there if it ever became impossible to earn his livelihood in the usual way at sea. When first he saw it it was drifting slowly, with the wind in the tops of the trees; but if the cable had not rusted away, it should be still where he left it, and they would make a rudder and hollow out cabins below, and at night they would hoist sails to the trunks of the trees and sail wherever they liked.

And all the pirates cheered, for they wanted to set their feet on land again somewhere where the hangman would not come and jerk them off it at once; and bold men though they were, it was a strain seeing so many lights coming their way at night. Even then . . . ! But it swerved away again and was lost in the mist.

And Captain Shard said that they would need to get provisions first, and he, for one, intended to marry before he settled down; and so they should have one more fight before they left the ship, and sack the sea-coast city Bombasharna and take from it provisions for several years, while he himself would marry the Queen of the South. And again the pirates cheered, for often they had seen sea-coast Bombasharna, and had always envied its opulence from the sea.

So they set all sail, and often altered their course, and dodged and fled from strange lights till dawn appeared, and all day long fled southwards. And by evening they saw the silver spires of slender Bombasharna, a city that was the glory of the coast. And in the midst of it, far away though they were, they saw the palace of the Queen of the South; and it was so full of windows all looking toward the sea, and they were so full of light, both from the sunset that was fading upon the water and from candles that maids were lighting one by one, that it looked far off like a pearl, shimmering still in its haliotis shell, still wet from the sea.

So Captain Shard and his pirates saw it, at evening over the water, and thought of rumours that said that Bombasharna was the loveliest city of the coasts of the world, and that its palace was lovelier even than Bombasharna; but for the Queen of the South rumour had no comparison. Then night came

down and hid the silver spires, and Shard slipped on through
the gathering darkness until by midnight the piratic ship lay
under the seaward battlements.

And at the hour when sick men mostly die, and sentries on
lonely ramparts stand to their arms, exactly half-an-hour
before dawn, Shard, with two rowing boats and half his crew,
with craftily muffled oars, landed below the battlements. They
were through the gateway of the palace itself before the alarm
was sounded, and as soon as they heard the alarm Shard's
gunners at sea opened upon the town, and, before the sleepy
soldiery of Bombasharna knew whether the danger was from
the land or the sea, Shard had successfully captured the
Queen of the South. They would have looted all day that silver
sea-coast city, but there appeared with dawn suspicious topsails just along the horizon. Therefore the captain with his
Queen went down to the shore at once and hastily re-
embarked and sailed away with what loot they had hurriedly
got, and with fewer men, for they had to fight a good deal to
get back to the boat. They cursed all day the interference of
those ominous ships which steadily grew nearer. There were
six ships at first, and that night they slipped away from all but
two; but all the next day those two were still in sight, and each
of them had more guns than the *Desperate Lark*. All the next
night Shard dodged about the sea, but the two ships separated
and one kept him in sight, and the next morning it was alone
with Shard on the sea, and his archipelago was just in sight,
the secret of his life.

And Shard saw he must fight, and a bad fight it was, and yet
it suited Shard's purpose, for he had more merry men when
the fight began than he needed for his island. And they got it
over before any other ship came up; and Shard put all adverse
evidence out of the way, and came that night to the islands
near the Sargasso Sea.

Long before it was light the survivors of the crew were peering at the sea, and when dawn came there was the island, no
bigger than two ships, straining hard at its anchor, with the
wind in the tops of the trees.

And then they landed and dug cabins below and raised the
anchor out of the deep sea, and soon they made the island
what they called shipshape. But the *Desperate Lark* they sent
away empty under full sail to sea, where more nations than
Shard suspected were watching for her, and where she was

presently captured by an admiral of Spain, who, when he found none of that famous crew on board to hang by the neck from the yard-arm, grew ill through disappointment.

And Shard on his island offered the Queen of the South the choicest of the old wines of Provence, and for adornment gave her Indian jewels looted from galleons with treasure for Madrid, and spread a table where she dined in the sun, while in some cabin below he bade the least coarse of his mariners sing; yet always she was morose and moody towards him, and often at evening he was heard to say that he wished he knew more about the ways of Queens. So they lived for years, the pirates mostly gambling and drinking below, Captain Shard trying to please the Queen of the South, and she never wholly forgetting Bombasharna. When they needed new provisions they hoisted sails on the trees, and as long as no ship came in sight they scudded before the wind, with the water rippling over the beach of the island; but as soon as they sighted a ship the sails came down, and they became an ordinary uncharted rock.

They mostly moved by night; sometimes they hovered off sea-coast towns as of old, sometimes they boldly entered river-mouths, and even attached themselves for a while to the mainland, whence they would plunder the neighbourhood and escape again to sea. And if a ship was wrecked on their island of a night they said it was all to the good. They grew very crafty in seamanship, and cunning in what they did, for they knew that any news of the *Desperate Lark*'s old crew would bring hangmen from the interior running down to every port.

And no one is known to have found them out or to have annexed their island; but a rumour arose and passed from port to port and every place where sailors meet together, and even survives to this day, of a dangerous uncharted rock anywhere between Plymouth and the Horn, which would suddenly rise in the safest track of ships, and upon which vessels were supposed to have been wrecked, leaving, strangely enough, no evidence of their doom. There was a little speculation about it at first, till it was silenced by the chance remark of a man old with wandering: "It is one of the mysteries that haunt the sea."

And almost Captain Shard and the Queen of the South lived happily ever after, though still at evening those on watch in the trees would see their captain sit with a puzzled air or hear him muttering now and again in a discontented way: "I wish I knew more about the ways of Queens."

Miss Cubbidge and the
Dragon of Romance

This tale is told in the balconies of Belgrave Square and among the towers of Pont Street; men sing it at evening in the Brompton Road.

Little upon her eighteenth birthday thought Miss Cubbidge, of Number 12A Prince of Wales' Square, that before another year had gone its way she would lose the sight of that unshapely oblong that was so long her home. And, had you told her further that within that year all trace of that so-called square, and of the day when her father was elected by a thumping majority to share in the guidance of the destinies of the empire, should utterly fade from her memory, she would merely have said in that affected voice of hers, "Go to!"

There was nothing about it in the daily Press, the policy of her father's party had no provision for it, there was no hint of it in conversation at evening parties to which Miss Cubbidge went: there was nothing to warn her at all that a loathsome dragon with golden scales that rattled as he went should have come up clean out of the prime of romance and gone by night (so far as we know) through Hammersmith, and come to Ardle Mansion, and then have turned to his left, which of course brought him to Miss Cubbidge's father's house.

There sat Miss Cubbidge at evening on her balcony quite alone, waiting for her father to be made a baronet. She was wearing walking-boots and a hat and a low-necked evening dress; for a painter was but just now painting her portrait and neither she nor the painter saw anything odd in the strange combination. She did not notice the roar of the dragon's golden scales, nor distinguish above the manifold lights of London the small, red glare of his eyes. He suddenly lifted his head, a blaze of gold, over the balcony; he did not appear a yellow dragon then, for his glistening scales reflected the beauty that London puts upon her only at evening and night. She screamed, but to no knight, nor knew what knight to call on, nor guessed where were the dragons' overthrowers of far, romantic days, nor what mightier game they chased, or what wars they waged; perchance they were busy even then arming for Armageddon.

Out of the balcony of her father's house in Prince of Wales' Square, the painted dark-green balcony that grew blacker every year, the dragon lifted Miss Cubbidge and spread his rattling wings, and London fell away like an old fashion. And England fell away, and the smoke of its factories, and the round material world that goes humming round the sun vexed and pursued by time, until there appeared the eternal and ancient lands of Romance lying low by mystical seas.

You had not pictured Miss Cubbidge stroking the golden head of one of the dragons of song with one hand idly, while with the other she sometimes played with pearls brought up from lonely places of the sea. They filled huge haliotis shells with pearls and laid them there beside her, they brought her emeralds which she set to flash among the tresses of her long black hair, they brought her threaded sapphires for her cloak: all this the princes of fable did and the elves and the gnomes of myth. And partly she still lived, and partly she was one with long-ago and with those sacred tales that nurses tell, when all their children are good, and evening has come, and the fire is burning well, and the soft pat-pat of the snow-flakes on the pane is like the furtive tread of fearful things in old, enchanted woods. If at first she missed those dainty novelties among which she was reared, the old, sufficient song of the mystical sea singing of faery lore at first soothed and at last consoled her. Even, she forgot those advertisements of pills that are so dear to England; even, she forgot political cant and the things that one discusses and the things that one does not, and had perforce to contend herself with seeing sailing by huge golden-laden galleons with treasure for Madrid, and the merry skull-and-crossbones of the pirateers, and the tiny nautilus setting out to sea, and ships of heroes trafficking in romance or of princes seeking for enchanted isles.

It was not by chains that the dragon kept her there, but by one of the spells of old. To one to whom the facilities of the daily Press had for so long been accorded spells would have palled—you would have said—and galleons after a time and all things out-of-date. After a time. But whether the centuries passed her or whether the years or whether no time at all, she did not know. If anything indicated the passing of time it was the rhythm of elfin horns blowing upon the heights. If the centuries went by her the spell that bound her gave her also perennial youth, and kept alight for ever the lantern by her side, and saved from decay the marble palace facing the mystical sea. And if no time went by her there at all, her single moment on those marvellous coasts was turned as it were to a crystal reflecting a thousand scenes. If it was all a dream, it was a dream that knew no morning and no fading away. The tide roamed on and whispered of mystery and of myth, while near that captive lady, asleep in his marble tank the golden dragon dreamed: and a little way out from the coast all that the dragon dreamed showed faintly in the mist that lay over the sea. He never dreamed of any rescuing knight. So long as he dreamed, it was twilight; but when he came up nimbly out of his tank night fell and starlight glistened on the dripping, golden scales.

There he and his captive either defeated Time or never encountered him at all; while, in the world we know, raged Roncesvalles or battles yet to be—I know not to what part of the shore of Romance he bore her. Perhaps she became one of those princesses of whom fable loves to tell, but let it suffice that there she lived by the sea: and kings ruled, and Demons ruled, and kings came again, and many cities returned to their native dust, and still she abided there, and still her marble palace passed not away nor the power that there was in the dragon's spell.

And only once did there ever come to her a message from the world that of old she knew. It came in a pearly ship across the mystical sea; it was from an old school-friend that she had had in Putney, merely a note, no more, in a little, neat, round hand: it said, "It is not Proper for you to be there alone."

The Quest of
the Queen's Tears

Sylvia, Queen of the Woods, in her woodland palace, held court, and made a mockery of her suitors. She would sing to them, she said, she would give them banquets, she would tell them tales of legendary days, her jugglers should caper before them, her armies salute them, her fools crack jests with them and make whimsical quips, only she could not love them.

This was not the way, they said, to treat princes in their splendour and mysterious troubadours concealing kingly names; it was not in accordance with fable; myth had no precedent for it. She should have thrown her glove, they said, into some lion's den, she should have asked for a score of venomous heads of the serpents of Licantara, or demanded the death of any notable dragon, or sent them all upon some deadly quest, but that she could not love them—! It was unheard of—it had no parallel in the annals of romance.

And then she said that if they must needs have a quest she would offer her hand to him who first should move her to tears: and the quest should be called, for reference in histories or song, the Quest of the Queen's Tears, and he that achieved them she would wed, be he only a petty duke of lands unknown to romance.

And many were moved to anger, for they hoped for some bloody quest; but the old lords chamberlain said, as they muttered among themselves in a far, dark end of the chamber, that the quest was hard and wise, for that if she could ever weep she might also love. They had known her all her childhood; she had never sighed. Many men had she seen, suitors and courtiers, and had never turned her head after one went by. Her beauty was as still sunsets of bitter evenings when all the world is frore, a wonder and a chill. She was as a sun-stricken mountain uplifted alone, all beautiful with ice, a desolate and lonely radiance late at evening far up beyond the comfortable world, not quite to be companioned by the stars, the doom of the mountaineer.

If she could weep, they said, she could love, they said.

And she smiled pleasantly on those ardent princes, and troubadours concealing kingly names.

Then one by one they told, each suitor prince the story of his love, with outstretched hands and kneeling on the knee; and very sorry and pitiful were the tales, so that often up in the galleries some maid of the palace wept. And very graciously she nodded her head like a listless magnolia in the deeps of the night moving idly to all the breezes its glorious bloom.

And when the princes had told their desperate loves and had departed away with no other spoil than of their own tears only, even then there came the unknown troubadours and told their tales in song, concealing their gracious names.

And one there was, Ackronnion, clothed with rags, on which was the dust of roads, and underneath the rags was war-scarred armour whereon were the dints of blows; and when he stroked his harp and sang his song, in gallery above gallery maidens wept, and even the old lords chamberlain whimpered among themselves and thereafter laughed through their tears and said: "It is easy to make old people weep and to bring idle tears from lazy girls; but he will not set a-weeping the Queen of the Woods."

And graciously she nodded, and he was the last. And disconsolate went away those dukes and princes, and troubadours in disguise. Yet Ackronnion pondered as he went away.

King he was of Afarmah, Lool and Haf, over-lord of Zeroora and hilly Chang, and duke of the dukedoms of Molong and Mlash, none of them unfamiliar with romance or unknown or overlooked in the making of myth. He pondered as he went in his thin disguise.

Now by those that do not remember their childhood, having other things to do, be it understood that underneath fairyland, which is, as all men know, at the edge of the world, there dwelleth the Gladsome Beast. A synonym he for joy.

It is known how the lark in its zenith, children at play out-of-doors, good witches and jolly old parents have all been compared—and how aptly!—with this very same Gladsome Beast. Only one "crab" he has (if I may use slang for a moment to make myself perfectly clear), only one drawback, and that is that in the gladness of his heart he spoils the cabbages of the

Old Man Who Looks After Fairyland,—and of course he eats men. It must further be understood that whoever may obtain the tears of the Gladsome Beast in a bowl, and become drunken upon them, may move all persons to shed tears of joy so long as he remains inspired by the potion to sing or to make music. Now Ackronnion pondered in this wise: that if he could obtain the tears of the Gladsome Beast by means of his art, withholding him from violence by the spell of music, and if a friend should slay the Gladsome Beast before his weeping ceased—for an end must come to weeping even with men— that so he might get safe away with the tears, and drink them before the Queen of the Woods and move her to tears of joy. He sought out therefore a humble knightly man who cared not for the beauty of Sylvia, Queen of the Woods, but had found a woodland maiden of his own once long ago in summer. And the man's name was Arrath, a subject of Ackronnion, a knight-at-arms of the spear-guard: and together they set out through the fields of fable until they came to Fairyland, a kingdom sunning itself (as all men know) for leagues along the edges of the world. And by a strange old pathway they came to the land they sought, through a wind blowing up the pathway sheer from space with a kind of metallic taste from the roving stars. Even so they came to the windy house of thatch where dwells the Old Man Who Looks After Fairyland sitting by parlour windows that look away from the world. He made them welcome in his star-ward parlour, telling them tales of Space, and when they named to him their perilous quest he said it would be a charity to kill the Gladsome Beast; for he was clearly one of these that liked not its happy ways. And then he took them out through his back door, for the front door had no pathway nor even a step—from it the old man used to empty his slops sheer on to the Southern Cross—and so they came to the garden wherein his cabbages were, and those flowers that only blow in Fairyland, turning their faces always towards the comet, and he pointed them out the way to the place he called Underneath, where the Gladsome Beast had his lair. Then they manoeuvered. Ackronnion was to go by the way of the steps with his harp and an agate bowl, while Arrath went round by a crag on the other side. Then the Old Man Who Looks After Fairyland went back to his windy house, muttering angrily as he passed his cabbages, for he did not love the

ways of the Gladsome Beast; and the two friends parted on
their separate ways.

Nothing perceived them but that ominous crow glutted over-
long already upon the flesh of man.

The wind blew bleak from the stars.

At first there was dangerous climbing, and then Ackronnion
gained the smooth broad steps that led from the edge to the
lair, and at that moment heard at the top of the steps the continuous chuckles of the Gladsome Beast.

He feared then that its mirth might be insuperable, not to be
saddened by the most grievous song; nevertheless he did not
turn back then, but softly climbed the stairs and, placing the
agate bowl upon a step, struck up the chaunt called Dolorous.
It told of desolate, regretted things befallen happy cities long
since in the prime of the world. It told of how the gods and
beasts and men had long ago loved beautiful companions, and
long ago in vain. It told of the golden host of happy hopes, but
not of their achieving. It told how Love scorned Death, but told
of Death's laughter. The contented chuckles of the Gladsome
Beast suddenly ceased in his lair. He rose and shook himself.
He was still unhappy. Ackronnion still sang on the chaunt
called Dolorous. The Gladsome Beast came mournfully up to
him. Ackronnion ceased not for the sake of his panic, but still
sang on. He sang of the malignity of time. Two tears welled
large in the eyes of the Gladsome Beast. Ackronnion moved
the agate bowl to a suitable spot with his foot. He sang of
autumn and of passing away. The beast wept as the frore hills
weep in the thaw, and the tears splashed big into the agate
bowl. Ackronnion desperately chaunted on; he told of the glad
unnoticed things men see and do not see again, of sunlight
beheld unheeded on faces now withered away. The bowl was
full. Ackronnion was desperate: the Beast was so close. Once
he thought that its mouth was watering!—but it was only the
tears that had run on the lips of the Beast. He felt as a morsel!
The Beast was ceasing to weep! He sang of worlds that had disappointed the gods. And all of a sudden, crash! and the
staunch spear of Arrath went home behind the shoulder, and
the tears and the joyful ways of the Gladsome Beast were
ended and over for ever.

And carefully they carried the bowl of tears away, leaving
the body of the Gladsome Beast as a change of diet for the ominous crow; and going by the windy house of thatch they said

farewell to the Old Man Who Looks After Fairyland, who when he heard of the deed rubbed his hands together and mumbled again and again, "And a very good thing, too. My cabbages! My cabbages!"

And not long after Ackronnion sang again in the sylvan palace of the Queen of the Woods, having first drunk all the tears in his agate bowl. And it was a gala night, and all the court were there and ambassadors from the lands of legend and myth, and even some from Terra Cognita.

And Ackronnion sang as he never sang before, and will not sing again. O, but dolorous, dolorous, are all the ways of man, few and fierce are his days, and the end trouble, and vain, vain his endeavor: and woman—who shall tell of it?—her doom is written with man's by listless, careless gods with their faces to other spheres.

Somewhat thus he began, and then inspiration seized him, and all the trouble in the beauty of his song may not be set down by me: there was much gladness in it, and all mingled with grief: it was like the way of man: it was like our destiny.

Sobs arose at his song, sighs came back along echoes: seneschals, soldiers, sobbed, and a clear cry made the maidens; like rain the tears came down from gallery to gallery.

All round the Queen of the Woods was a storm of sobbing and sorrow.

But no, she would not weep.

The Hoard of
the Gibbelins

The Gibbelins eat, as is well known, nothing less good than man. Their evil tower is joined to Terra Cognita, to the lands we know, by a bridge. Their hoard is beyond reason; avarice has no use for it; they have a separate cellar for emeralds and a separate cellar for sapphires; they have filled a hole with gold and dig it up when they need it. And the only use that is known for their ridiculous wealth is to attract to their larder a continual supply of food. In times of famine they have even been known to scatter rubies abroad, a little trail of them to some city of Man, and sure enough their larders would soon be full again.

Their tower stands on the other side of that river known to Homer—ὁ ῥόος ἀχεανοίο, as he called it—which surrounds the world. And where the river is narrow and fordable the tower was built by the Gibbelins' gluttonous sires, for they liked to see burglars rowing easily to their steps. Some nourishment that common soil has not the huge trees drained there with their colossal roots from both banks of the river.

There the Gibbelins lived and discreditably fed.

Alderic, Knight of the Order of the City and the Assault, hereditary Guardian of the King's Peace of Mind, a man not unremembered among the makers of myth, pondered so long upon the Gibbelins' hoard that by now he deemed it his. Alas that I should say of so perilous a venture, undertaken at dead of night by a valorous man, that its motive was sheer avarice! Yet upon avarice only the Gibbelins relied to keep their larders full, and once in every hundred years sent spies into the cities of men to see how avarice did, and always the spies returned again to the tower saying that all was well.

It may be thought that, as the years went on and men came by fearful ends on that tower's wall, fewer and fewer would come to the Gibbelins' table: but the Gibbelins found otherwise.

Not in the folly and frivolity of his youth did Alderic come to the tower, but he studied carefully for several years the manner in which burglars met their doom when they went in search of the treasure that he considered his. *In every case they had entered by the door.*

He consulted those who gave advice on this quest; he noted every detail and cheerfully paid their fees, and determined to do nothing that they advised, for what were their clients now? No more than examples of the savoury art, mere half-forgotten memories of a meal; and many, perhaps, no longer even that.

These were the requisites for the quest that these men used to advise: a horse, a boat, mail armour, and at least three men-at-arms. Some said, "Blow the horn at the tower door"; others said, "Do not touch it."

Alderic thus decided: he would take no horse down to the river's edge, he would not row along it in a boat, and he would go alone and by way of the Forest Unpassable.

How pass, you may say, the unpassable? This was his plan: there was a dragon he knew of who if peasants' prayers are heeded deserved to die, not alone because of the number of maidens he cruelly slew, but because he was bad for the crops; he ravaged the very land and was the bane of a dukedom.

Now Alderic determined to go up against him. So he took horse and spear and pricked till he met the dragon, and the dragon came out against him breathing bitter smoke. And to him Alderic shouted, "Hath foul dragon ever slain true knight?" And well the dragon knew that this had never been, and he hung his head and was silent, for he was glutted with blood. "Then," said the knight, "if thou would'st ever taste maiden's blood again thou shalt be my trusty steed, and if not, by this spear there shall befall thee all that the troubadours tell of the dooms of thy breed."

And the dragon did not open his ravening mouth, nor rush upon the knight, breathing out fire; for well he knew the fate of those that did these things, but he consented to the terms imposed, and swore to the knight to become his trusty steed.

It was on a saddle upon this dragon's back that Alderic afterwards sailed above the unpassable forest, even above the tops of those measureless trees, children of wonder. But first he pondered that subtle plan of his which was more profound than merely to avoid all that had been done before; and he commanded a blacksmith, and the blacksmith made him a pickaxe.

Now there was great rejoicing at the rumour of Alderic's quest, for all folk knew that he was a cautious man, and they deemed that he would succeed and enrich the world, and they rubbed their hands in the cities at the thought of largesse; and there was joy among all men in Alderic's country, except perchance among the lenders of money, who feared they would soon be paid. And there was rejoicing also because men hoped that when the Gibbelins were robbed of their hoard, they would shatter their high-built bridge and break the golden chains that bound them to the world, and drift back, they and their tower, to the moon, from which they had come and to which they rightly belonged. There was little love for the Gibbelins, though all men envied their hoard.

So they all cheered, that day when he mounted his dragon, as though he was already a conqueror, and what pleased them more than the good that they hoped he would do to the world was that he scattered gold as he rode away; for he would not need it, he said, if he found the Gibbelins' hoard, and he would not need it more if he smoked on the Gibbelins' table.

When they heard that he had rejected the advice of those that gave it, some said that the knight was mad, and others said he was greater than those that gave the advice, but none appreciated the worth of his plan.

He reasoned thus: for centuries men had been well advised and had gone by the cleverest way, while the Gibbelins came to expect them to come by boat and to look for them at the door whenever their larder was empty, even as a man looketh for a snipe in the marsh; but how, said Alderic, if a snipe should sit in the top of a tree, and would men find him there? Assuredly never! So Alderic decided to swim the river and not to go by the door, but to pick his way into the tower through the stone. Moreover, it was in his mind to work below the level of the ocean, the river (as Homer knew) that girdles the world, so that as soon as he made a hole in the wall the water should pour in, confounding the Gibbelins, and flooding the cellars rumoured to be twenty feet in depth, and therein he would dive for emeralds as a diver dives for pearls.

And on the day that I tell of he galloped away from his home scattering largesse of gold, as I have said, and passed through many kingdoms, the dragon snapping at maidens as he went, but being unable to eat them because of the bit in his mouth, and earning no gentler reward than a spurthrust where he was softest. And so they came to the swart arboreal precipice of the unpassable forest. The dragon rose at it with a rattle of wings. Many a farmer near the edge of the worlds saw him up there where yet the twilight lingered, a faint, black, wavering line; and mistaking him for a row of geese going inland from the ocean, went into their houses cheerily rubbing their hands and saying that winter was coming, and that we should soon have snow. Soon even there the twilight faded away, and when they descended at the edge of the world it was night and the moon was shining. Ocean, the ancient river, narrow and shallow there, flowed by and made no murmur. Whether the Gibbelins banqueted or whether they watched by the door, they also made no murmur. And Alderic dismounted and took his armour off, and saying one prayer to his lady, swam with his pickaxe. He did not part from his sword, for fear that he meet with a Gibbelin. Landed the other side, he began to work at once, and all went well with him. Nothing put out its head from any window, and all were lighted so that nothing within could see him in the dark. The blows of his pickaxe were dulled in the deep walls. All night he worked, no sound came to molest him, and at dawn the last rock swerved and tumbled inwards, and the river poured in after. Then Alderic took a stone, and went to the bottom step, and hurled the stone at the door; he heard the echoes roll into the tower, then he ran back and dived through the hole in the wall.

He was in the emerald-cellar. There was no light in the lofty vault above him, but, diving through twenty feet of water, he felt the floor all rough with emeralds, and open coffers full of them. By a faint ray of the moon he saw that the water was green with them, and, easily filling a satchel, he rose again to the surface; and there were the Gibbelins waist-deep in the water, with torches in their hands! And, without saying a word, *or even smiling,* they neatly hanged him on the outer wall—and the tale is one of those that have not a happy ending.

How Nuth Would Have Practised His Art Upon the Gnoles

Despite the advertisements of rival firms, it is probable that every tradesman knows that nobody in business at the present time has a position equal to that of Mr. Nuth. To those outside the magic circle of business, his name is scarcely known; he does not need to advertise, he is consummate. He is superiour even to modern competition, and, whatever claims they boast, his rivals know it. His terms are moderate, so much cash down when the goods are delivered, so much in blackmail afterwards. He consults your convenience. His skill may be counted upon; I have seen a shadow on a windy night move more noisily than Nuth, for Nuth is a burglar by trade. Men have been known to stay in country houses and to send a dealer afterwards to bargain for a piece of tapestry that they saw there—some article of furniture, some picture. This is bad taste: but those whose culture is more elegant invariably send Nuth a night or two after their visit. He has a way with tapestry; you would scarcely notice that the edges had been cut. And often when I see some huge, new house full of old furniture and portraits from other ages, I say to myself, "These mouldering chairs, these full-length ancestors and carved mahogany are the produce of the incomparable Nuth."

It may be urged against my use of the word incomparable that in the burglary business the name of Slith stands paramount and alone; and of this I am not ignorant; but Slith is a classic, and lived long ago, and knew nothing at all of modern competition; besides which the surprising nature of his doom has possibly cast a glamour upon Slith that exaggerates in our eyes his undoubted merits.

It must not be thought that I am any friend of Nuth's, on the contrary such politics as I have are on the side of Property; and he needs no words from me, for his position is almost unique in trade, being among the very few that do not need to advertise.

At the time that my story begins Nuth lived in a roomy

36

house in Belgrave Square: in his inimitable way he had made friends with the caretaker. The place suited Nuth, and, whenever anyone came to inspect it before purchase, the caretaker used to praise the house in the words that Nuth had suggested. "If it wasn't for the drains," she would say, "it's the finest house in London," and when they pounced on this remark and asked questions about the drains, she would answer them that the drains also were good, but not so good as the house. They did not see Nuth when they went over the rooms, but Nuth was there.

Here in a neat black dress on one spring morning came an old woman whose bonnet was lined with red, asking for Mr. Nuth; and with her came her large and awkward son. Mrs. Eggins, the caretaker, glanced up the street, and then she let them in, and left them to wait in the drawing-room amongst furniture all mysterious with sheets. For a long while they waited, and then there was a smell of pipe-tobacco, and there was Nuth standing quite close to them.

"Lord," said the old woman whose bonnet was lined with red, "you did make me start." And then she saw by his eyes that that was not the way to speak to Mr. Nuth.

And at last Nuth spoke, and very nervously the old woman explained that her son was a likely lad, and had been in business already but wanted to better himself, and she wanted Mr. Nuth to teach him a livelihood.

First of all Nuth wanted to see a business reference, and when he was shown one from a jeweller with whom he happened to be hand-in-glove the upshot of it was that he agreed to take young Tonker (for this was the surname of the likely lad) and to make him his apprentice. And the old woman whose bonnet was lined with red went back to her little cottage in the country, and every evening said to her old man, "Tonker, we must fasten the shutters of a night-time, for Tommy's a burglar now."

The details of the likely lad's apprenticeship I do not propose to give; for those that are in the business know those details already, and those that are in other businesses care only for their own, while men of leisure who have no trade at all would fail to appreciate the gradual degrees by which Tommy Tonker came first to cross bare boards, covered with little obstacles in the dark, without making any sound, and then to go silently up creaky stairs, and then to open doors, and lastly to climb.

Let it suffice that the business prospered greatly, while glowing reports of Tommy Tonker's progress were sent from time to time to the old woman whose bonnet was lined with red in the laborious handwriting of Nuth. Nuth had given up lessons in writing very early, for he seemed to have some prejudice against forgery, and therefore considered writing a waste of time. And then there came the transaction with Lord Castlenorman at his Surrey residence. Nuth selected a Saturday night, for it chanced that Saturday was observed as Sabbath in the family of Lord Castlenorman, and by eleven o'clock the whole house was quiet. Five minutes before midnight Tommy Tonker, instructed by Mr. Nuth, who waited outside, came away with one pocketful of rings and shirt-studs. It was quite a light pocketful, but the jewellers in Paris could not match it without sending specially to Africa, so that Lord Castlenorman had to borrow bone shirt-studs.

Not even rumour whispered the name of Nuth. Were I to say that this turned his head, there are those to whom the assertion would give pain, for his associates hold that his astute judgment was unaffected by circumstance. I will say, therefore, that it spurred his genius to plan what no burglar had ever planned before. It was nothing less than to burgle the house of the gnoles. And this that abstemious man unfolded to Tonker over a cup of tea. Had Tonker not been nearly insane with pride over their recent transaction, and had he not been blinded by a veneration for Nuth, he would have—but I cry over spilt milk. He expostulated respectfully: he said he would rather not go; he said it was not fair, he allowed himself to argue; and in the end, one windy October morning with a menace in the air found him and Nuth drawing near to the dreadful wood.

Nuth, by weighing little emeralds against pieces of common rock, had ascertained the probable weight of those house-ornaments that the gnoles are believed to possess in the narrow, lofty house wherein they have dwelt from of old. They decided to steal two emeralds and to carry them between them on a cloak; but if they should be too heavy one must be dropped at once. Nuth warned young Tonker against greed, and explained that the emeralds were worth less than cheese until they were safe away from the dreadful wood.

Everything had been planned, and they walked now in silence.

No track led up to the sinister gloom of the trees, either of men or cattle; not even a poacher had been there snaring elves for over a hundred years. You did not trespass twice in the dells of the gnoles. And, apart from the things that were done there, the trees themselves were a warning, and did not wear the wholesome look of those that we plant ourselves.

The nearest village was some miles away with the backs of all its houses turned to the wood, and without one window at all facing in that direction. They did not speak of it there, and elsewhere it is unheard of.

Into this wood stepped Nuth and Tommy Tonker. They had no firearms. Tonker had asked for a pistol, but Nuth replied that the sound of a shot "would bring everything down on us," and no more was said about it.

Into the wood they went all day, deeper and deeper. They saw the skeleton of some early Georgian poacher nailed to a door in an oak tree; sometimes they saw a fairy scuttle away from them; once Tonker stepped heavily on a hard, dry stick, after which they both lay still for twenty minutes. And the sunset flared full of omens through the tree trunks, and night fell, and they came by fitful starlight, as Nuth had foreseen, to that lean, high house where the gnoles so secretly dwelt.

All was so silent by that unvalued house that the faded courage of Tonker flickered up, but to Nuth's experienced sense it seemed too silent; and all the while there was that look in the sky that was worse than a spoken doom, so that Nuth, as is often the case when men are in doubt, had leisure to fear the worst. Nevertheless he did not abandon the business, but sent the likely lad with the instruments of his trade by means of the ladder to the old green casement. And the moment that Tonker touched the withered boards, the silence that, though ominous, was earthly, became unearthly like the touch of a ghoul. And Tonker heard his breath offending against that silence, and his heart was like mad drums in a night attack, and a string of one of his sandals went tap on a rung of a ladder, and the leaves of the forest were mute, and the breeze of the night was still; and Tonker prayed that a mouse or a mole might make any noise at all, but not a creature stirred, even Nuth was still. And then and there, while yet he was undiscovered, the likely lad made up his mind, as he should have done long before, to leave those colossal emeralds where they were and have nothing further to do with the lean, high house of the gnoles, but to quit this

sinister wood in the nick of time and retire from business at
once and buy a place in the country. Then he descended softly
and beckoned to Nuth. But the gnoles had watched him
through knavish holes that they bore in trunks of the trees,
and the unearthly silence gave way, as it were with a grace, to
the rapid screams of Tonker as they picked him up from
behind—screams that came faster and faster until they were
incoherent. And where they took him it is not good to ask, and
what they did with him I shall not say.

Nuth looked on for a while from the corner of the house with
a mild surprise on his face as he rubbed his chin, for the trick
of the holes in the trees was new to him; then he stole nimbly
away through the dreadful wood.

"And did they catch Nuth?" you ask me, gentle reader.

"Oh, no, my child" (for such a question is childish). "Nobody
ever catches Nuth."

How One Came,
as Was Foretold,
to the City of Never

The child that played about the terraces and gardens in sight of the Surrey hills never knew that it was he that should come to the Ultimate City, never knew that he should see the Under Pits, the barbicans and the holy minarets of the mightiest city known. I think of him now as a child with a little red watering-can going about the gardens on a summer's day that lit the warm south country, his imagination delighted with all tales of quite little adventures, and all the while there was reserved for him that feat at which men wonder.

Looking in other directions, away from the Surrey hills, through all his infancy he saw that precipice that, wall above wall and mountain above mountain, stands at the edge of the World, and in perpetual twilight alone with the Moon and the Sun holds up the inconceivable City of Never. To tread its streets he was destined; prophecy knew it. He had the magic halter, and a worn old rope it was; an old wayfaring woman had given it to him: it had the power to hold any animal whose race had never known captivity, such as the unicorn, the hippogriff Pegasus, dragons and wyverns; but with a lion, giraffe, camel or horse, it was useless.

How often we have seen that City of Never, that marvel of the Nations! Not when it is night in the World, and we can see no further than the stars; not when the sun is shining where we dwell, dazzling our eyes; but when the sun has set on some stormy days, all at once repentant at evening, and those glittering cliffs reveal themselves which we almost take to be clouds, and it is twilight with us as it is for ever with them, then on their gleaming summits we see those golden domes that overpeer the edges of the World and seem to dance with dignity and calm in that gentle light of evening that is Wonder's native haunt. Then does the City of Never, unvisited and afar, look long at her sister the World.

41

It had been prophecied that he should come there. They knew it when the pebbles were being made and before the isles of coral were given unto the sea. And thus the prophecy came unto fulfilment and passed into history, and so at length to Oblivion, out of which I drag it as it goes floating by, into which I shall one day tumble. The hippogriffs dance before dawn in the upper air; long before sunrise flashes upon our lawns they go to glitter in light that has not yet come to the World, and as the dawn works up from the ragged hills and the stars feel it they go slanting earthwards, till sunlight touches the tops of the tallest trees, and the hippogriffs alight with a rattle of quills and fold their wings and gallop and gambol away till they come to some prosperous, wealthy, detestable town, and they leap at once from the fields and soar away from the sight of it, pursued by the horrible smoke of it until they come again to the pure blue air.

He whom prophecy had named from of old to come to the City of Never, went down one midnight with his magic halter to a lake-side where the hippogriffs alighted at dawn, for the turf was soft there and they could gallop far before they came to a town, and there he waited hidden near their hoofmarks. And the stars paled a little and grew indistinct; but there was no other sign as yet of the dawn, when there appeared far up in the deeps of the night two little saffron specks, then four and five: it was the hippogriffs dancing and twirling around in the sun. Another flock joined them, there were twelve of them now; they danced there, flashing their colours back to the sun, they descended in wide curves slowly; trees down on earth revealed against the sky, jet-black each delicate twig; a star disappeared from a cluster, now another; and dawn came on like music, like a new song. Ducks shot by to the lake from still dark fields of corn, far voices uttered, a colour grew upon water, and still the hippogriffs gloried in the light, revelling up in the sky; but when pigeons stirred on the branches and the first small bird was abroad, and little coots from the rushes ventured to peer about, then there came down on a sudden with a thunder of feathers the hippogriffs, and, as they landed from their celestial heights all bathed with the day's first sunlight, the man whose destiny it was as from of old to come to the City of Never, sprang up and caught the last with the magic halter. It plunged, but could not escape it, for the hippogriffs are of the uncaptured races, and magic has power over the magical, so the man mounted it, and it soared again for the heights whence it had come, as a

wounded beast goes home. But when they came to the heights
that venturous rider saw huge and fair to the left of him the destined City of Never, and he beheld the towers of Lel and Lek,
Neerib and Akathooma, and the cliffs of Toldenarba a-glistening
in the twilight like an alabaster statue of the Evening. Towards
them he wrenched the halter, towards Toldenarba and the
Under Pits; the wings of the hippogriff roared as the halter
turned him. Of the Under Pits who shall tell? Their mystery is
secret. It is held by some that they are the sources of night, and
that darkness pours from them at evening upon the world; while
others hint that knowledge of these might undo our civilization.

There watched him ceaselessly from the Under Pits those
eyes whose duty it is; from further within and deeper, the bats
that dwell there arose when they saw the surprise in the eyes;
the sentinels on the bulwarks beheld that stream of bats and
lifted up their spears as it were for war. Nevertheless when they
perceived that that war for which they watched was not now
come upon them, they lowered their spears and suffered him to
enter, and he passed whirring through the earthward gateway.
Even so he came, as foretold, to the City of Never perched upon
Toldenarba, and saw late twilight on those pinnacles that know
no other light. All the domes were of copper, but the spires on
their summits were gold. Little steps of onyx ran all this way
and that. With cobbled agates were its streets a glory. Through
small square panes of rose-quartz the citizens looked from their
houses. To them as they looked abroad the World far-off seemed
happy. Clad though that city was in one robe always, in twilight,
yet was its beauty worthy of even so lovely a wonder: city and
twilight both were peerless but for each other. Built of a stone
unknown in the world we tread were its bastions, quarried we
know not where, but called by the gnomes *abyx,* it so flashed
back to the twilight its glories, colour for colour, that none can
say of them where their boundary is, and which the eternal twilight, and which the City of Never; they are the twin-born children, the fairest daughters of Wonder. Time had been there, but
not to work destruction; he had turned to a fair pale green the
domes that were made of copper, the rest he had left untouched,
even he, the destroyer of cities, by what bribe I know not
averted. Nevertheless they often wept in Never for change and
passing away, mourning catastrophes in other worlds, and they
built temples sometimes to ruined stars that had fallen flaming
down from the Milky Way, giving them worship still when by us

long since forgotten. Other temples they have—who knows to what divinities?

And he that was destined alone of men to come to the City of Never was well content to behold it as he trotted down its agate street, with the wings of his hippogriff furled, seeing at either side of him marvel on marvel of which even China is ignorant. Then as he neared the city's further rampart by which no inhabitant stirred, and looked in a direction to which no houses faced with any rose-pink windows, he suddenly saw far-off, dwarfing the mountains, an even greater city. Whether that city was built upon the twilight or whether it rose from the coasts of some other world he did not know. He saw it dominate the City of Never, and strove to reach it; but at this unmeasured home of unknown colossi the hippogriff shied frantically, and neither the magic halter nor anything that he did could make the monster face it. At last, from the City of Never's lonely outskirts where no inhabitants walked, the rider turned slowly earthwards, he knew now why all the windows faced this way—the denizens of the twilight gazed at the world and not at a greater than them. Then from the last step of the earthward stairway, like lead past the Under Pits and down the glittering face of Toldenarba, down from the overshadowed glories of the gold-tipped City of Never and out of perpetual twilight, swooped the man on his winged monster: the wind that slept at the time leaped up like a dog at their onrush, it uttered a cry and ran past them. Down on the World it was morning; night was roaming away with his cloak trailed behind him, white mists turned over and over as he went, the orb was grey but it glittered, lights blinked surprisingly in early windows, forth over wet, dim fields went cows from their houses: even in this hour touched the fields again the feet of the hippogriff. And the moment that the man dismounted and took off his magic halter the hippogriff flew slanting away with a whirr, going back to some airy dancing-place of his people.

And he that surmounted glittering Toldenarba and came alone of men to the City of Never has his name and his fame among nations; but he and the people of that twilit city well know two things unguessed by other men, they that there is another city fairer than theirs, and he—a deed unaccomplished.

The Coronation of Mr. Thomas Shap

It was the occupation of Mr. Thomas Shap to persuade customers that the goods were genuine and of an excellent quality, and that as regards the price their unspoken will was consulted. And in order to carry on this occupation he went by train very early every morning some few miles nearer to the City from the suburb in which he slept. This was the use to which he put his life.

From the moment when he first perceived (not as one reads a thing in a book, but as truths are revealed to one's instinct) the very beastliness of his occupation, and of the house that he slept in, its shape, make and pretensions, and of even the clothes that he wore; from that moment he withdrew his dreams from it, his fancies, his ambitions, everything in fact except that ponderable Mr. Shap that dressed in a frock-coat, bought tickets and handled money and could in turn be handled by the statistician. The priest's share in Mr. Shap, the share of the poet, never caught the early train to the City at all.

He used to take little flights of fancy at first, dwelt all day in his dreamy way on fields and rivers lying in the sunlight where it strikes the world more brilliantly further South. And then he began to imagine butterflies there; after that, silken people and the temples they built to their gods.

They noticed that he was silent, and even absent at times, but they found no fault with his behaviour with customers, to whom he remained as plausible as of old. So he dreamed for a year, and his fancy gained strength as he dreamed. He still read halfpenny papers in the train, still discussed the passing day's ephemeral topic, still voted at elections, though he no longer did these things with the whole Shap—his soul was no longer in them.

He had had a pleasant year, his imagination was all new to him still, and it had often discovered beautiful things away where it went, southeast at the edge of the twilight. And he had a matter-of-fact and logical mind, so that he often said, "Why should I pay my twopence at the electric theatre when I can see all sorts of things quite easily without?" Whatever he

45

did was logical before anything else, and those that knew him always spoke of Shap as "a sound, sane, level-headed man."

On far the most important day of his life he went as usual to town by the early train to sell plausible articles to customers, while the spiritual Shap roamed off to fanciful lands. As he walked from the station, dreamy but wide awake, it suddenly struck him that the real Shap was not the one walking to Business in black and ugly clothes, but he who roamed along a jungle's edge near the ramparts of an old and Eastern city that rose up sheer from the sand, and against which the desert lapped with one eternal wave. He used to fancy the name of that city was Larkar. "After all, the fancy is as real as the body," he said with perfect logic. It was a dangerous theory.

For that other life that he led he realized, as in Business, the importance and value of method. He did not let his fancy roam too far until it perfectly knew its first surroundings. Particularly he avoided the jungle—he was not afraid to meet a tiger there (after all it was not real), but stranger things might crouch there. Slowly he built up Larkar: rampart by rampart, towers for archers, gateway of brass, and all. And then one day he argued, and quite rightly, that all the silk-clad people in its streets, their camels, their wares that came from Inkustahn, the city itself, were all the things of his will—and then he made himself King. He smiled after that when people did not raise their hats to him in the street, as he walked from the station to Business; but he was sufficiently practical to recognize that it was better not to talk of this to those that only knew him as Mr. Shap.

Now that he was King in the city of Larkar and in all the desert that lay to the East and North he sent his fancy to wander further afield. He took the regiments of his camel-guard and went jingling out of Larkar, with little silver bells under the camels' chins, and came to other cities far-off on the yellow sand, with clear white walls and towers, uplifting themselves in the sun. Through their gates he passed with his three silken regiments, the light-blue regiment of the camel-guard being upon his right and the green regiment riding at his left, the lilac regiment going on before. When he had gone through the streets of any city and observed the ways of its people, and had seen the way that the sunlight struck its towers, he would proclaim himself King there, and then ride on in fancy. So he passed from city to city and from land to land. Clear-sighted though Mr. Shap was, I think he overlooked the lust of aggrandizement to which kings have so often been victims: and so it was that when the first few cities had opened their gleaming gates and he saw peoples prostrate before his camel, and spearmen cheering along countless balconies, and priests come out to do him reverence, he that had never had even the lowliest authority in the familiar world became unwisely insatiate. He let his fancy ride at inordinate speed, he forsook method, scarce was he king of a land but he yearned to extend his borders; so he journeyed deeper and deeper into the wholly unknown. The concentration that he gave to this inordinate progress through countries of which history is ignorant and cities so fantastic in their bulwarks that, though their inhabitants were human, yet the foe that they feared seemed something less or more; the amazement with which he beheld gates and towers unknown even to art, and furtive people thronging intricate ways to acclaim him as their sovereign; all these things began to affect his capacity for Business. He knew as well as any that his fancy could not rule these beautiful lands unless that other Shap, however unimportant, were well sheltered and fed: and shelter and food meant money, and money, Business. His was more like the mistake of some gambler with cunning schemes who overlooks human greed. One day his fancy, riding in the morning, came to a city gorgeous as the sunrise, in whose opalescent wall were gates of gold, so huge that a river poured between the bars, floating in, when the gates were opened, large galleons under sail. Thence there came dancing out a company with instruments, and made a melody all round the wall; that morning Mr. Shap, the bodily Shap in London, forgot the train to town.

Until a year ago he had never imagined at all; it is not to be wondered at that all these things now newly seen by his fancy should play tricks at first with the memory of even so sane a man. He gave up reading the papers altogether, he lost all interest in politics, he cared less and less for things that were going on around him. This unfortunate missing of the morning train even occurred again, and the firm spoke to him severely about it. But he had his consolation. Were not Aráthrion and Argun Zeerith and all the level coasts of Oora his? And even as the firm found fault with him his fancy watched the yaks on weary journeys, slow specks against the snow-fields, bringing tribute; and saw the green eyes of the mountain men who had looked at him strangely in the city of Nith when he had entered it by the desert door. Yet his logic did not forsake him; he knew well that his strange subjects did not exist, but he was prouder of having created them with his brain, than merely of ruling them only; thus in his pride he felt himself something more great than a king, he did not dare to think what! He went into the temple of the city of Zorra and stood some time there alone: all the priests kneeled to him when he came away.

He cared less and less for the things we care about, for the affairs of Shap, the business-man in London. He began to despise the man with a royal contempt.

One day when he sat in Sowla, the city of the Thuls, throned on one amethyst, he decided, and it was proclaimed on the moment by silver trumpets all along the land, that he would be crowned as king over all the lands of Wonder.

By that old temple where the Thuls worshipped, year in, year out, for over a thousand years, they pitched pavilions in the open air. The trees that blew there threw out radiant scents unknown in any countries that know the map; the stars blazed fiercely for that famous occasion. A fountain hurled up, clattering, ceaselessly into the air armfuls on armfuls of diamonds, a deep hush waited for the golden trumpets, the holy coronation night was come. At the top of those old, worn steps, going down we know not whither, stood the king in the emerald-and-amethyst cloak, the ancient garb of the Thuls; beside him lay that Sphinx that for the last few weeks had advised him in his affairs.

Slowly, with music when the trumpets sounded, came up towards him from we know not where, one-hundred-and-twenty archbishops, twenty angels and two archangels, with that terrific crown, the diadem of the Thuls. They knew as they came up to him that promotion awaited them all because of this night's work. Silent, majestic, the king awaited them.

The doctors downstairs were sitting over their supper, the warders softly slipped from room to room, and when in that cosy dormitory of Hanwell they saw the king still standing erect and royal, his face resolute, they came up to him and addressed him: "Go to bed," they said—"pretty bed." So he lay down and soon was fast asleep: the great day was over.

Chu-bu and Sheemish

It was the custom on Tuesdays in the temple of Chu-bu for the priests to enter at evening and chant, "There is none but Chu-bu."

And all the people rejoiced and cried out, "There is none but Chu-bu." And honey was offered to Chu-bu, and maize and fat. Thus was he magnified.

Chu-bu was an idol of some antiquity, as may be seen from the colour of the wood. He had been carved out of mahogany, and after he was carved he had been polished. Then they had set him up on the diorite pedestal with the brazier in front of it for burning spices and the flat gold plates for fat. Thus they worshipped Chu-bu.

He must have been there for over a hundred years when one day the priests came in with another idol into the temple of Chu-bu, and set it up on a pedestal near Chu-bu's and sang, "There is also Sheemish."

And all the people rejoiced and cried out, "There is also Sheemish."

Sheemish was palpably a modern idol, and although the wood was stained with a dark-red dye, you could see that he had only just been carved. And honey was offered to Sheemish as well as Chu-bu, and also maize and fat.

The fury of Chu-bu knew no time-limit; he was furious all that night, and next day he was furious still. The situation called for immediate miracles. To devastate the city with a pestilence and kill all his priests was scarcely within his power, therefore he wisely concentrated such divine powers as he had in commanding a little earthquake. "Thus," thought Chu-bu, "will I reassert myself as the only god, and men shall spit upon Sheemish."

Chu-bu willed it and willed it and still no earthquake came, when suddenly he was aware that the hated Sheemish was daring to attempt a miracle too. He ceased to busy himself about the earthquake and listened, or shall I say felt, for what

Sheemish was thinking; for gods are aware of what passes in the mind by a sense that is other than any of our five. Sheemish was trying to make an earthquake too.

The new god's motive was probably to assert himself. I doubt if Chu-bu understood or cared for his motive; it was sufficient for an idol already aflame with jealousy that his detestable rival was on the verge of a miracle. All the power of Chu-bu veered round at once and set dead against an earthquake, even a little one. It was thus in the temple of Chu-bu for some time, and then no earthquake came.

To be a god and to fail to achieve a miracle is a despairing sensation; it is as though among men one should determine upon a hearty sneeze and as though no sneeze should come; it is as though one should try to swim in heavy boots or remember a name that is utterly forgotten: all these pains were Sheemish's.

And upon Tuesday the priests came in, and the people, and they did worship Chu-bu and offered fat to him, saying, "O Chu-bu who made everything," and then the priests sang, "There is also Sheemish"; and Chu-bu was put to shame and spake not for three days.

Now there were holy birds in the temple of Chu-bu, and when the third day was come and the night thereof, it was as it were revealed to the mind of Chu-bu, that there was dirt upon the head of Sheemish.

And Chu-bu spake unto Sheemish as speak the gods, moving no lips nor yet disturbing the silence, saying, "There is dirt upon thy head, O Sheemish." All night long he muttered again and again, "there is dirt upon Sheemish's head." And when it was dawn and voices were heard far off, Chu-bu became exultant with Earth's awakening things, and cried out till the sun was high, "Dirt, dirt, dirt, upon the head of Sheemish," and at noon he said, "So Sheemish would be a god." Thus was Sheemish confounded.

And with Tuesday one came and washed his head with rosewater, and he was worshipped again when they sang "There is also Sheemish." And yet was Chu-bu content, for he said, "The head of Sheemish has been defiled," and again, "His head was defiled, it is enough." And one evening lo! there was dirt on the head of Chu-bu also, and the thing was perceived of Sheemish.

It is not with the gods as it is with men. We are angry one with another and turn from our anger again, but the wrath of the gods is enduring. Chu-bu remembered and Sheemish did not forget. They spake as we do not speak, in silence yet heard of each other, nor were their thoughts as our thoughts. We should not judge them by merely human standards. All night long they spake and all night said these words only: "Dirty Chu-bu," "Dirty Sheemish." "Dirty Chu-bu," "Dirty Sheemish," all night long. Their wrath had not tired at dawn, and neither had wearied of his accusation. And gradually Chu-bu came to realize that he was nothing more than the equal of Sheemish. All gods are jealous, but this equality with the upstart Sheemish, a thing of painted wood a hundred years newer than Chu-bu, and this worship given to Sheemish in Chu-bu's own temple, were particularly bitter. Chu-bu was jealous even for a god; and when Tuesday came again, the third day of Sheemish's worship, Chu-bu could bear it no longer. He felt that his anger must be revealed at all costs, and he returned with all the vehemence of his will to achieving a little earth-quake. The worshippers had just gone from his temple when Chu-bu settled his will to attain this miracle. Now and then his meditations were disturbed by that now familiar dictum, "Dirty Chu-bu," but Chu-bu willed ferociously, not even stop-ping to say what he longed to say and had already said nine hundred times, and presently even these interruptions ceased.

They ceased because Sheemish had returned to a project that he had never definitely abandoned, the desire to assert himself and exalt himself over Chu-bu by performing a mira-cle, and the district being volcanic he had chosen a little earth-quake as the miracle most easily accomplished by a small god.

Now an earthquake that is commanded by two gods has dou-ble the chance of fulfilment than when it is willed by one, and an incalculably greater chance than when two gods are pulling different ways; as, to take the case of older and greater gods, when the sun and the moon pull in the same direction we have the biggest tides.

Chu-bu knew nothing of the theory of tides, and was too much occupied with his miracle to notice what Sheemish was doing. And suddenly the miracle was an accomplished thing.

It was a very local earthquake, for there are other gods than Chu-bu or even Sheemish, and it was only a little one as the gods had willed, but it loosened some monoliths in a colonnade that supported one side of the temple and the whole of one wall fell in, and the low huts of the people of that city were shaken a little and some of their doors were jammed so that they would not open; it was enough, and for a moment it seemed that it was all; neither Chu-bu nor Sheemish commanded there should be more, but they had set in motion an old law older than Chu-bu, the law of gravity that that colonnade had held back for a hundred years, and the temple of Chu-bu quivered and then stood still, swayed once and was overthrown, on the heads of Chu-bu and Sheemish.

No one rebuilt it, for nobody dared to near such terrible gods. Some said that Chu-bu wrought the miracle, but some said Sheemish, and thereof schism was born; the weakly amiable, alarmed by the bitterness of rival sects, sought compromise and said that both had wrought it, but no one guessed the truth that the thing was done in rivalry.

And a saying arose, and both sects held this belief in common, that whoso toucheth Chu-bu shall die or whoso looketh upon Sheemish.

That is how Chu-bu came into my possession when I travelled once beyond the hills of Ting. I found him in the fallen temple of Chu-bu with his hands and toes sticking up out of the rubbish, lying upon his back, and in that attitude just as I found him I keep him to this day on my mantelpiece, as he is less liable to be upset that way. Sheemish was broken, so I left him where he was.

And there is something so helpless about Chu-bu with his fat hands stuck up in the air that sometimes I am moved out of compassion to bow down to him and pray, saying, "O Chu-bu, thou that made everything, help thy servant."

Chu-bu cannot do much, though once I am sure that at a game of bridge he sent me the ace of trumps after I had not held a card worth having for the whole of the evening. And chance could have done as much as that for me, but I do not tell this to Chu-bu.

The Wonderful Window

The old man in the Oriental-looking robe was being moved on by the police, and it was this that attracted to him and the parcel under his arm the attention of Mr. Sladden, whose livelihood was earned in the emporium of Messrs. Mergin and Chater, that is to say in their establishment.

Mr. Sladden had the reputation of being the silliest young man in Business; a touch of romance—a mere suggestion of it—would send his eyes gazing away as though the walls of the emporium were of gossamer and London itself a myth, instead of attending to customers.

Merely the fact that the dirty piece of paper that wrapped the old man's parcel was covered with Arabic writing was enough to give Mr. Sladden the ideas of romance, and he followed until the little crowd fell off and the stranger stopped by the kerb and unwrapped his parcel and prepared to sell the thing that was inside it. It was a little window in old wood with small panes set in lead; it was not much more than a foot in breadth and was under two feet long. Mr. Sladden had never before seen a window sold in the street, so he asked the price of it.

"Its price is all you possess," said the old man.

"Where did you get it?" said Mr. Sladden, for it was a strange window.

"I gave all that I possessed for it in the streets of Baghdad."

"Did you possess much?" said Mr. Sladden.

"I had all that I wanted," he said, "except this window."

"It must be a good window," said the young man.

"It is a magical window," said the old one.

"I have only ten shillings on me, but I have fifteen-and-six at home."

The old man thought for a while.

"Then twenty-five-and-sixpence is the price of the window," he said.

It was only when the bargain was completed and the ten

53

shillings paid and the strange old man was coming for his fifteen-and-six and to fit the magical window into his only room that it occurred to Mr. Sladden's mind that he did not want a window. And then they were at the door of the house in which he rented a room, and it seemed too late to explain.

The stranger demanded privacy when he fitted up the window, so Mr. Sladden remained outside the door at the top of a little flight of creaky stairs. He heard no sound of hammering.

And presently the strange old man came out with his faded yellow robe and his great beard, and his eyes on far-off places. "It is finished," he said, and he and the young man parted. And whether he remained a spot of colour and an anachronism in London, or whether he ever came again to Baghdad, and what dark hands kept on the circulation of his twenty-five-and-six, Mr. Sladden never knew.

Mr. Sladden entered the bare-boarded room in which he slept and spent all his indoor hours between closing-time and the hour at which Messrs. Mergin and Chater commenced. To the Penates of so dingy a room his neat frock-coat must have been a continual wonder. Mr. Sladden took it off and folded it carefully; and there was the old man's window rather high up in the wall. There had been no window in that wall hitherto, nor any ornament at all but a small cupboard, so when Mr. Sladden had put his frock-coat safely away he glanced through his new window. It was where his cupboard had been in which he kept his tea-things: they were all standing on the table now. When Mr. Sladden glanced through his new window it was late in a summer's evening; the butterflies some while ago would have closed their wings, though the bat would scarcely yet be drifting abroad—but this was in London: the shops were shut and street-lamps not yet lighted.

Mr. Sladden rubbed his eyes, then rubbed the window, and still he saw a sky of blazing blue, and far, far down beneath him, so that no sound came up from it or smoke of chimneys, a mediæval city set with towers. Brown roofs and cobbled streets, and then white walls and buttresses, and beyond them bright green fields and tiny streams. On the towers archers lolled, and along the walls were pikemen, and now and then a wagon went down some old-world street and lumbered through the gateway and out to the country, and now and then a wagon drew up to the city from the mist that was rolling with evening over the fields. Sometimes folk put their heads out of lattice windows, sometimes some idle troubadour seemed to sing, and nobody hurried or troubled about anything. Airy and dizzy though the distance was, for Mr. Sladden seemed higher above the city than any cathedral gargoyle, yet one clear detail he obtained as a clue: the banners floating from every tower over the idle archers had little golden dragons all over a pure white field.

He heard motor-buses roar by his other window, he heard the newsboys howling.

Mr. Sladden grew dreamier than ever after that on the premises, in the establishment of Messrs. Mergin and Chater. But in one matter he was wise and wakeful: he made continuous and careful inquiries about the golden dragons on a white flag, and talked to no one of his wonderful window. He came to know the flags of every king in Europe, he even dabbled in history, he made inquiries at shops that understood heraldry, but nowhere could he learn any trace of little dragons *or* on a field *argent*. And when it seemed that for him alone those golden dragons had fluttered he came to love them as an exile in some desert might love the lilies of his home or as a sick man might love swallows when he cannot easily live to another spring.

As soon as Messrs. Mergin and Chater closed, Mr. Sladden used to go back to his dingy room and gaze through the wonderful window until it grew dark in the city and the guard would go with a lantern round the ramparts and the night came up like velvet, full of strange stars. Another clue he tried to obtain one night by jotting down the shapes of the constellations, but this led him no further, for they were unlike any that shone upon either hemisphere.

Each day as soon as he woke he went first to the wonderful window, and there was the city, diminutive in the distance, all shining in the morning, and the golden dragons dancing in the sun, and the archers stretching themselves or swinging their arms on the tops of the windy towers. The window would not open, so that he never heard the songs that the troubadours sang down there beneath the gilded balconies; he did not even hear the belfries' chimes, though he saw the jackdaws routed every hour from their homes. And the first thing that he always did was to cast his eye round all the little towers that rose up from the ramparts to see that the little golden dragons were flying there on their flags. And when he saw them flaunting themselves on white folds from every tower against the marvelous deep blue of the sky he dressed contentedly, and, taking one last look, went off to his work with a glory in his mind. It would have been difficult for the customers of Messrs. Mergin and Chater to guess the precise ambition of Mr. Sladden as he walked before them in his neat frock-coat: it was that he might be a man-at-arms or an archer in order to fight for the little golden dragons that flew on a white flag for an unknown king in an inaccessible city. At first Mr. Sladden used to walk round and round the mean street that he lived in, but he gained no clue from that; and soon he noticed that quite different winds blew below his wonderful window from those that blew on the other side of the house.

In August the evenings began to grow shorter: this was the very remark that the other employees made to him at the emporium, so that he almost feared that they suspected his secret, and he had much less time for the wonderful window, for lights were few down there and they blinked out early.

One morning late in August, just before he went to Business, Mr. Sladden saw a company of pikemen running down the cobbled road towards the gateway of the mediæval city—Golden Dragon City he used to call it alone in his own mind, but he never spoke of it to anyone. The next thing that he noticed was that the archers on the towers were talking a good deal together and were handling round bundles of arrows in addition to the quivers which they wore. Heads were thrust out of windows more than usual, a woman ran out and called some children indoors, a knight rode down the street, and then more pikemen appeared along the walls, and all the jackdaws were in the air. In the street no troubadour sang. Mr. Sladden took one look along the towers to see that the flags were flying, and all the golden dragons were streaming in the wind. Then he had to go to Business. He took a 'bus back that evening and ran upstairs. Nothing seemed to be happening in Golden Dragon City except a crowd in the cobbled street that led down to the gateway; the archers seemed to be reclining as usual lazily in their towers, then a white flag went down with all its golden dragons; he did not see at first that all the archers were dead. The crowd was pouring towards him, towards the precipitous wall from which he looked; men with a white flag covered with golden dragons were moving backwards slowly, men with another flag were pressing them, a flag on which there was one huge red bear. Another banner went down upon a tower. Then he saw it all: the golden dragons were being beaten—his little golden dragons. The men of the bear were coming under the window; whatever he threw from that height would fall with terrific force: fire-irons, coal, his clock, whatever he had—he would fight for his little golden dragons yet. A flame broke out from one of the towers and licked the feet of a reclining archer; he did not stir. And now the alien standard was out of sight directly underneath. Mr. Sladden broke the panes of the wonderful window and wrenched away with a poker the lead that held them. Just as the glass broke he saw a banner covered with golden dragons fluttering still, and then as he drew back to hurl the poker there came to him the scent of mysterious spices, and there was nothing there, not even the daylight, for behind the fragments of the wonderful window was nothing but that small cupboard in which he kept his tea-things.

And though Mr. Sladden is older now and knows more of the world, and even has a Business of his own, he has never been able to buy such another window, and has not ever since, either from books or men, heard any rumour at all of Golden Dragon City.

Epilogue

Here the fourteenth Episode of the Book of Wonder endeth and here the relating of the Chronicles of Little Adventures at the Edge of the World. I take farewell of my readers. But it may be we shall even meet again, for it is still to be told how the gnomes robbed the fairies, and of the vengeance that the fairies took, and how even the gods themselves were troubled thereby in their sleep; and how the King of Ool insulted the troubadours, thinking himself safe among his scores of archers and hundreds of halberdiers, and how the troubadours stole to his towers by night, and under his battlements by the light of the moon made that king ridiculous for ever in song. But for this I must first return to the Edge of the World. Behold, the caravans start.

Tales of Wonder

Preface

THESE tales are tales of peace. Those who
remember peace and those who will see it
again may be glad to turn their eyes, though
but for a moment, away from a world of mud
and blood and khaki, and to read for a while
of cities too good to be true.

A Tale of London

"Come," said the Sultan to his hasheesh-eater in the very furthest lands that know Bagdad, "dream to me now of London."

And the hasheesh-eater made a low obeisance and seated himself cross-legged upon a purple cushion broidered with golden poppies, on the floor, beside an ivory bowl where the hasheesh was, and having eaten liberally of the hasheesh blinked seven times and spoke thus:

"O Friend of God, know then that London is the desiderate town even of all Earth's cities. Its houses are of ebony and cedar which they roof with thin copper plates that the hand of Time turns green. They have golden balconies in which amethysts are, where they sit and watch the sunset. Musicians in the gloaming steal softly along the ways; unheard their feet fall on the white sea-sand with which those ways are strewn, and in the darkness suddenly they play on dulcimers and instruments with strings. Then are there murmurs in the balconies praising their skill, then are there bracelets cast down to them for reward, and golden necklaces, and even pearls.

"Indeed but the city is fair; there is by the sandy ways a paving all alabaster, and the lanterns along it are of chrysoprase; all night long they shine green, but of amethyst are the lanterns of the balconies.

"As the musicians go along the ways dancers gather about them and dance upon the alabaster pavings, for joy and not for hire. Sometimes a window opens far up in an ebony palace and a wreath is cast down to a dancer or orchids showered upon them.

"Indeed of many cities have I dreamt, but of none fairer; through many marble metropolitan gates hasheesh has led me, but London is its secret, the last gate of all; the ivory bowl has nothing more to show. And indeed even now the imps that crawl behind me, and that will not let me be, are plucking me by the elbow and bidding my spirit return, for well they know that I have seen too much. 'No, not London,' they say; and therefore I will speak of some other city, a city of some less mysterious land, and anger not the imps with forbidden things. I will speak of Persepolis or famous Thebes."

A shade of annoyance crossed the Sultan's face, a look of thunder that you had scarcely seen, but in those lands they watched his visage well; and though his spirit was wandering far away and his eyes were bleared with hasheesh, yet that story-teller there and then perceived the look that was death, and sent his spirit back at once to London as a man runs into his house when the thunder comes.

"And therefore," he continued, "in the desiderate city, in London, all their camels are pure white. Remarkable is the swiftness of their horses, that draw their chariots that are of ivory along those sandy ways and that are of surpassing lightness; they have little bells of silver upon their horses' heads. O Friend of God, if you perceived their merchants! The glory of their dresses in the noonday! They are no less gorgeous than those butterflies that float about their streets. They have overcloaks of green and vestments of azure, huge purple flowers blaze on their overcloaks, the work of cunning needles; the centres of the flowers are of gold and the petals of purple. All their hats are black——" ("No, no," said the Sultan)—"but irises are set about the brims, and green plumes float above the crowns of them.

"They have a river that is named the Thames, on it their ships go up with violet sails bringing incense for the braziers that perfume the streets, new songs exchanged for gold with alien tribes, raw silver for the statues of their heroes, gold to make balconies where their women sit, great sapphires to reward their poets with, the secrets of old cities and strange lands, the learning of the dwellers in far isles, emeralds, diamonds and the hoards of the sea. And whenever a ship comes into port and furls its violet sails and the news spreads through London that she has come, then all the merchants go down to the river to barter, and all day long the chariots whirl through the streets, and the sound of their going is a mighty roar all day until evening, their roar is even like . . ."

"Not so," said the Sultan.

"Truth is not hidden from the Friend of God," replied the hasheesh-eater. "I have erred, being drunken with hasheesh; for in the desiderate city, even in London, so thick upon the ways is the white sea-sand, with which the city glimmers, that no sound comes from the path of the charioteers, but they go softly like a light sea-wind . . ." ("It is well," said the Sultan.) "They go softly down to the port where the vessels are, and the merchandise in from the sea, amongst the wonders that the sailors show, on land by the high ships, and softly they go though swiftly at evening back to their homes.

"O would that the Munificent, the Illustrious, the Friend of God, had even seen these things, had seen the jewellers with their empty baskets, bargaining there by the ships, when the barrels of emeralds came up from the hold. Or would that he had seen the fountains there in silver basins in the midst of the ways. I have seen small spires upon their ebony houses and the spires were all of gold, birds strutted there upon the copper roofs from golden spire to spire that have no equal for splendour in all the woods of the world. And over London the desiderate city the sky is so deep a blue that by this alone the traveller may know where he has come, and may end his fortunate journey. Nor yet for any colour of the sky is there too great heat in London, for along its ways a wind blows always from the South, gently and cools the city.

"Such, O Friend of God, is indeed the city of London, lying very far off on the yonder side of Bagdad, without a peer for beauty or excellence of its ways among all the towns of the earth or cities of song; and even so, as I have told, its fortunate citizens dwell, with their hearts ever devising beautiful things and from the beauty of their own fair work that is more abundant around them every year, receiving new inspiration to work things more beautiful yet."

"And is their government good?" the Sultan said.

"It is most good," said the hasheesh-eater, and fell backwards upon the floor.

He lay thus and was silent. And when the Sultan perceived he would speak no more that night he smiled and lightly applauded.

And there was envy in that palace, in lands beyond Bagdad, of all that dwell in London.

Thirteen at Table

In front of a spacious fire-place of the old kind, when the logs were well alight, and men with pipes and glasses were gathered before it in great easeful chairs, and the wild weather outside and the comfort that was within, and the season of the year—for it was Christmas—and the hour of the night, all called for the weird or uncanny, then out spoke the ex-master of foxhounds and told this tale.

"I once had an odd experience too. It was when I had the Bromley and Sydenham, the year I gave them up—as a matter of fact it was the last day of the season. It was no use going on because there were no foxes left in the country, and London was sweeping down on us. You could see it from the kennels all along the skyline like a terrible army in grey, and masses of villas every year came skirmishing down our valleys. Our coverts were mostly on the hills, and as the town came down upon the valleys the foxes used to leave them and go right away out of the country, and they never returned. I think they went by night and moved great distances. Well, it was early April and we had drawn blank all day, and at the last draw of all, the very last of the season, we found a fox. He left the covert with his back to London and its railways and villas and wire, and slipped away towards the chalk country and open Kent. I felt as I once felt as a child on one summer's day when I found a door in a garden where I played left luckily ajar, and I pushed it open and the wide lands were before me and waving fields of corn.

"We settled down into a steady gallop and the fields began to drift by under us, and a great wind arose full of fresh breath. We left the clay lands where the bracken grows and came to a valley at the edge of the chalk. As we went down into it we saw the fox go up the other side like a shadow that crosses the evening, and glide into a wood that stood on the top. We saw a flash of primroses in the wood and we were out on the other side, hounds hunting perfectly and the fox still going

64

absolutely straight. It began to dawn on me then that we were
in for a great hunt; I took a deep breath when I thought of it;
the taste of the air that perfect spring afternoon as it came to
one galloping, and the thought of a great run, were together
like some old rare wine. Our faces now were to another valley,
large fields led down to it with easy hedges, at the bottom of it
a bright blue stream went singing and a rambling village
smoked, the sunlight on the opposite slopes danced like a fairy;
and all along the top old woods were frowning, but they
dreamed of spring. The field had fallen off and were far behind
and my only human companion was James, my old first whip,
who had a hound's instinct, and a personal animosity against
a fox that even embittered his speech.

"Across the valley the fox went as straight as a railway line,
and again we went without a check straight through the woods
at the top. I remember hearing men sing or shout as they
walked home from work, and sometimes children whistled; the
sounds came up from the village to the woods at the top of the
valley. After that we saw no more villages, but valley after valley arose and fell before us as though we were voyaging some
strange and stormy sea; and all the way before us the fox went
dead up-wind like the fabulous flying Dutchman. There was no
one in sight now but my first whip and me; we had both of us
got on to our second horses as we drew the last covert. Two or
three times we checked in those great lonely valleys beyond
the village, but I began to have inspirations; I felt a strange
certainty within me that this fox was going on straight up-
wind till he died or until night came and we could hunt no
longer, so I reversed ordinary methods and only cast straight
ahead, and always we picked up the scent again at once. I
believe that this fox was the last one left in the villa-haunted
lands and that he was prepared to leave them for remote
uplands far from men, that if we had come the following day
he would not have been there, and that we just happened to hit
off his journey.

"Evening began to descend upon the valleys, still the hounds
drifted on, like the lazy but unresting shadows of clouds upon
a summer's day; we heard a shepherd calling to his dog, we
saw two maidens move toward a hidden farm, one of them
singing softly; no other sounds but ours disturbed the leisure
and the loneliness of haunts that seemed not yet to have
known the inventions of steam and gunpowder.

"And now the day and our horses were wearing out, but that resolute fox held on. I began to work out the run and to wonder where we were. The last landmark I had ever seen before must have been over five miles back, and from there to the start was at least ten miles more. If only we could kill! Then the sun set. I wondered what chance we had of killing our fox. I looked at James' face as he rode beside me. He did not seem to have lost any confidence, yet his horse was as tired as mine. It was a good clear twilight and the scent was as strong as ever, and the fences were easy enough, but those valleys were terribly trying, and they still rolled on and on. It looked as if the light would outlast all possible endurance both of the fox and the horses, if the scent held good and he did not go to ground, otherwise night would end it. For long we had seen no houses and no roads, only chalk slopes with the twilight on them, and here and there some sheep, and scattered copses darkening in the evening. At some moment I seemed to realize all at once that the light was spent and that darkness was hovering. I looked at James, he was solemnly shaking his head. Suddenly in a little wooded valley we saw climb over the oaks the red-brown gables of a queer old house; at that instant I saw the fox scarcely leading by fifty yards. We blundered through a wood into full sight of the house, but no avenue led up to it or even a path, nor were there any signs of wheelmarks anywhere. Already lights shone here and there in windows. We were in a park, and a fine park, but unkempt beyond credibility; brambles grew everywhere. It was too dark to see the fox any more, but we knew he was dead-beat, the hounds were just before us—and a four-foot railing of oak. I shouldn't have tried it on a fresh horse at the beginning of a run, and here was a horse near his last gasp, but what a run! an event standing out in a life-time, and the hounds, close up on their fox, slipping into the darkness as I hesitated. I decided to try it. My horse rose about eight inches and took it fair with his breast, and the oak log flew into handfuls of wet decay,—it was rotten with years. And then we were on a lawn, and at the far end of it the hounds were tumbling over their fox. Fox, horses, and light were all done together at the end of a twenty-mile point. We made some noise then, but nobody came out of the queer old house.

"I felt pretty stiff as I walked round to the hall door with the mask and the brush, while James went with the hounds and the two horses to look for the stables. I rang a bell marvellously encrusted with rust, and after a long while the door opened a little way, revealing a hall with much old armour in it and the shabbiest butler that I have ever known.

"I asked him who lived there. Sir Richard Arlen. I explained that my horse could go no further that night, and that I wished to ask Sir Richard Arlen for a bed.

"'O, no one ever comes here, sir,' said the butler.

"I pointed out that I had come.

"'I don't think it would be possible, sir,' he said.

"This annoyed me, and I asked to see Sir Richard, and insisted until he came. Then I apologized and explained the situation. He looked only fifty, but a 'Varsity oar on the wall with the date of the early seventies made him older than that; his face had something of the shy look of the hermit; he regretted that he had not room to put me up. I was sure that this was untrue, also I had to be put up there, there was nowhere else within miles, so I almost insisted. Then, to my astonishment, he turned to the butler and they talked it over in an undertone. At last they seemed to think that they could manage it, though clearly with reluctance. It was by now seven o'clock, and Sir Richard told me he dined at half-past seven. There was no question of clothes for me other than those I stood in, as my host was shorter and broader. He showed me presently to the drawing-room, and then he reappeared before half-past seven in evening dress and a white waistcoat. The drawing-room was large and contained old furniture, but it was rather worn than venerable; an aubusson carpet flapped about the floor, the wind seemed momently to enter the room, and old draughts haunted corners; stealthy feet of rats that were never at rest indicated the extent of the ruin that time had wrought in the wainscot, somewhere far off a shutter flapped to and fro, the guttering candles were insufficient to light so large a room. The gloom that these things suggested was quite in keeping with Sir Richard's first remark to me after he entered the room.

"'I must tell you, sir, that I have led a wicked life. O, a very wicked life.'

"Such confidences from a man much older than oneself after one has known him for half an hour are so rare that any possible answer merely does not suggest itself. I said rather slowly, 'O, really,' and chiefly to forestall another such remark, I said, 'What a charming house you have.'

"'Yes,' he said, 'I have not left it for nearly forty years. Since I

left the 'Varsity. One is young there, you know, and one has opportunities; but I make no excuses, no excuses.' And the door slipping
its rusty latch, came drifting on the draught into the room, and
the long carpet flapped and the hangings upon the walls, then the
draught fell rustling away and the door slammed to again.

"'Ah, Marianne,' he said. 'We have a guest to-night. Mr.
Linton. This is Marianne Gib.' And everything became clear to
me. 'Mad,' I said to myself, for no one had entered the room.

"The rats ran up the length of the room behind the wainscot
ceaselessly, and the wind unlatched the door again and the
folds of the carpet fluttered up to our feet and stopped there,
for our weight held it down.

"'Let me introduce Mr. Linton,' said my host. 'Lady Mary
Errinjer.'

"The door slammed back again. I bowed politely. Even had I
been invited I should have humoured him, but it was the very
least that an uninvited guest could do.

"This kind of thing happened eleven times, the rustling, and
the fluttering of the carpet, and the footsteps of the rats, and
the restless door, and then the sad voice of my host introduc-
ing me to phantoms. Then for some while we waited while I
struggled with the situation; conversation flowed slowly. And
again the draught came trailing up the room, while the flaring
candles filled it with hurrying shadows. 'Ah, late again, Cicely,'
said my host in his soft mournful way. 'Always late, Cicely.'
Then I went down to dinner with that man and his mind and
the twelve phantoms that haunted it. I found a long table with
fine old silver on it, and places laid for fourteen. The butler
was now in evening dress, there were fewer draughts in the
dining-room, the scene was less gloomy there. 'Will you sit next
to Rosalind at the other end?' Sir Richard said to me. 'She
always takes the head of the table. I wronged her most of all.'

"I said, 'I shall be delighted.'

"I looked at the butler closely; but never did I see by any
expression of his face, or by anything that he did, any suggestion that he waited upon less than fourteen people in the complete possession of all their faculties. Perhaps a dish appeared
to be refused more often than taken, but every glass was
equally filled with champagne. At first I found little to say, but
when Sir Richard, speaking from the far end of the table, said,
'You are tired, Mr. Linton?' I was reminded that I owed something to a host upon whom I had forced myself. It was excel-

lent champagne, and with the help of a second glass I made the effort to begin a conversation with a Miss Helen Errold, for whom the place upon one side of me was laid. It came more easy to me very soon; I frequently paused in my monologue, like Mark Antony, for a reply, and sometimes I turned and spoke to Miss Rosalind Smith. Sir Richard at the other end talked sorrowfully on; he spoke as a condemned man might speak to his judge, and yet somewhat as a judge might speak to one that he once condemned wrongly. My own mind began to turn to mournful things. I drank another glass of champagne, but I was still thirsty. I felt as if all the moisture in my body had been blown away over the downs of Kent by the wind up which we had galloped. Still I was not talking enough: my host was looking at me. I made another effort; after all I had something to talk about: a twenty-mile point is not often seen in a lifetime, especially south of the Thames. I began to describe the run to Rosalind Smith. I could see then that my host was pleased, the sad look in his face gave a kind of a flicker, like mist upon the mountains on a miserable day when a faint puff comes from the sea and the mist would lift if it could. And the butler refilled my glass very attentively. I asked her first if she hunted, and paused and began my story. I told her where we found the fox and how fast and straight he had gone, and how I had got through the village by keeping to the road, while the little gardens and wire, and then the river, had stopped the rest of the field. I told her the kind of country that we crossed and how splendid it looked in the spring, and how mysterious the valleys were as soon as the twilight came, and what a glorious horse I had and how wonderfully he went.

"I was so fearfully thirsty after the great hunt that I had to stop for a moment now and then, but I went on with my description of that famous run, for I had warmed to the subject, and after all there was nobody to tell of it but me except my old whipper-in, and 'the old fellow's probably drunk by now' I thought. I described to her minutely the exact spot in the run at which it had come to me clearly that this was going to be the greatest hunt in the whole history of Kent. Sometimes I forgot incidents that had happened, as one well may in a run of twenty miles, and then I had to fill in the gaps by inventing. I was pleased to be able to make the party go off well by means of my conversation, and besides that the lady to whom I was speaking was extremely pretty: I do not mean in a flesh-and-blood kind of way, but there were little shadowy lines about the chair beside me that hinted at an unusually graceful figure when Miss Rosalind Smith was alive; and I began to perceive that what I first mistook for the smoke of guttering candles and a tablecloth waving in the draught was in reality an extremely animated company who listened, and not without interest, to my story of by far the greatest hunt that the world had ever known: indeed, I told them that I would confidently go further and predict that never in the history of the world would there be such a run again. Only my throat was terribly dry.

"And then, as it seemed, they wanted to hear more about my horse. I had forgotten that I had come there on a horse, but when they reminded me it all came back; they looked so charming leaning over the table, intent upon what I said, that I told them everything they wanted to know. Everything was going so pleasantly if only Sir Richard would cheer up. I heard his mournful voice every now and then—these were very pleasant people if only he would take them the right way. I could understand that he regretted his past, but the early seventies seemed centuries away, and I felt now that he misunderstood these ladies, they were not revengeful as he seemed to suppose. I wanted to show him how cheerful they really were, and so I made a joke and they all laughed at it, and then I chaffed them a bit, especially Rosalind, and nobody resented it in the very least. And still Sir Richard sat there with that unhappy look, like one that has ended weeping because it is vain and has not the consolation even of tears.

"We had been a long time there, and many of the candles had burnt out, but there was light enough. I was glad to have an audience for my exploit, and being happy myself I was determined Sir Richard should be. I made more jokes and they still laughed good-naturedly; some of the jokes were a little broad perhaps, but no harm was meant. And then,—I do not wish to excuse myself, but I had had a harder day than I ever had had before, and without knowing it I must have been completely exhausted; in this state the champagne had found me, and what would have been harmless at any other time must somehow have got the better of me when quite tired out. Anyhow, I went too far, I made some joke,—I cannot in the least remember what,—that suddenly seemed to offend them. I felt all at once a commotion in the air; I looked up and saw that they had all risen from the table and were sweeping towards the door. I had not time to open it, but it blew open on a wind; I could scarcely see what Sir Richard was doing because only two candles were left, I think the rest blew out when the ladies suddenly rose. I sprang up to apologize, to assure them—and then fatigue overcame me as it had overcome my horse at the last fence, I clutched at the table, but the cloth came away, and then I fell. The fall, and the darkness on the floor, and the pent-up fatigue of the day overcame me all three together.

"The sun shone over glittering fields and in at a bedroom window, and thousands of birds were chaunting to the spring, and there I was in an old four-poster bed in a quaint old pan-elled bedroom, fully dressed, and wearing long muddy boots; someone had taken my spurs and that was all. For a moment I failed to realize, and then it all came back—my enormity and the pressing need of an abject apology to Sir Richard. I pulled an embroidered bell-rope until the butler came; he came in perfectly cheerful and indescribably shabby. I asked him if Sir Richard was up, and he said he had just gone down, and told me to my amazement that it was twelve o'clock. I asked to be shown in to Sir Richard at once.

"He was in his smoking-room. 'Good morning,' he said cheer-fully the moment I went in. I went directly to the matter in hand. 'I fear that I insulted some ladies in your house . . .' I began.

"'You did indeed,' he said. 'You did indeed.' And then he burst into tears, and took me by the hand. 'How can I ever thank you?' he said to me then. 'We have been thirteen at table for thirty years, and I never dared to insult them because I had wronged them all, and now you have done it, and I know they will never dine here again.' And for a long time he still held my hand, and then he gave it a grip and a kind of a shake which I took to mean 'good-bye,' and I drew my hand away then and left the house. And I found James in the disused stables with the hounds and asked him how he had fared, and James, who is a man of very few words, said he could not rightly remem-ber, and I got my spurs from the butler and climbed on to my horse; and slowly we rode away from that queer old house, and slowly we wended home, for the hounds were foot-sore but happy and the horses were tired still. And when we recalled that the hunting season was ended, we turned our faces to spring and thought of the new things that try to replace the old. And that very year I heard, and have often heard since, of dances and happier dinners at Sir Richard Arlen's house."

The City on
Mallington Moor

Besides the old shepherd at Langside, whose habits render him unreliable, I am probably the only person that has ever seen the city on Mallington Moor.

I had decided one year to do no London season, partly because of the ugliness of the things in the shops, partly because of the unresisted invasion of German bands, partly perhaps because some pet parrots in the oblong where I lived had learnt to imitate cab-whistles, but chiefly because of late there had seized me in London a quite unreasonable longing for large woods and waste spaces, while the very thought of little valleys underneath copses full of bracken and foxgloves was a torment to me, and every summer in London the longing grew worse till the thing was becoming intolerable. So I took a stick and a knapsack and began walking northwards, starting at Tetherington and sleeping at inns, where one could get real salt and the waiter spoke English, and where one had a name instead of a number; and though the tablecloth might be dirty, the windows opened so that the air was clean; where one had the excellent company of farmers and men of the wold, who could not be thoroughly vulgar because they had not the money to be so even if they had wished it. At first the novelty was delightful, and then one day in a queer old inn up Uthering way beyond Langside I heard for the first time the rumour of the city said to be on Mallington Moor. They spoke of it quite casually over their glasses of beer, two farmers at the inn. "They say the queer folk be at Mallington with their city," one farmer said. "Travelling they seem to be," said the other. And more came in then and the rumour spread. And then, such are the contradictions of our little likes and dislikes and all the whims that drive us, that I who had come so far to avoid cities had a great longing all of a sudden for throngs again and the great hives of Man, and then and there determined on that bright Sunday morning to come to Mallington and there search for the city that rumour spoke of so strangely.

Mallington Moor from all that they said of it was hardly a likely place to find a thing by searching. It was a huge high moor, very bleak and desolate, and altogether trackless. It seemed a lonely place from what they said. The Normans when they came had called it Mal Lieu, and afterwards Mallieutown, and so it changed to Mallington. Though what a town can ever have had to do with a place so utterly desolate I do not know. And before that some say that the Saxons called it Baplas, which I believe to be a corruption of Bad Place.

And beyond the mere rumour of a beautiful city all of white marble and with a foreign look up on Mallington Moor, beyond this I could not get. None of them had seen it themselves, "only heard of it like," and my questions rather than stimulating conversation would always stop it abruptly. I was no more fortunate on the road to Mallington, until the Tuesday when I was quite near it; I had been walking two days from the inn where I had heard the rumour and could see the great hill, steep as a headland, on which Mallington lay, standing up on the skyline: the hill was covered with grass, where anything grew at all, but Mallington Moor is all heather; it is just marked Moor on the map; nobody goes there and they do not trouble to name it. It was there where the gaunt hill first came into sight, by the roadside as I enquired for the marble city of some labourers by the way, that I was directed, partly I think in derision, to the old shepherd of Langside. It appeared that he, following sometimes sheep that had strayed, and wandering far from Langside, came sometimes up to the edge of Mallington Moor, and that he would come back from these excursions and shout through the villages, raving of a city of white marble and gold-tipped minarets. And hearing me asking questions of this city they had laughed and directed me to the shepherd of Langside. One well-meant warning they gave me as I went—the old man was not reliable.

And late that evening I saw the thatches of Langside sheltering under the edge of that huge hill that Atlas-like held up those miles of moor to the great winds and heaven.

They knew less of the city in Langside than elsewhere, but they knew the whereabouts of the man I wanted, though they seemed a little ashamed of him. There was an inn in Langside that gave me shelter, whence in the morning equipped with purchases I set out to find their shepherd. And there he was on the edge of Mallington Moor standing motionless, gazing stu-

pidly at his sheep; his hands trembled continually and his eyes
had a blear look, but he was quite sober, wherein all Landside
had wronged him.

And then and there I asked him of the city, and he said he
had never heard tell of any such place. And I said, "Come,
come, you must pull yourself together." And he looked angrily
at me; but when he saw me draw from amongst my purchases
a full bottle of whiskey and a big glass he became more
friendly. As I poured out the whiskey I asked him again about
the marble city on Mallington Moor, but he seemed quite hon-
estly to know nothing about it. The amount of whiskey he
drank was quite incredible, but I seldom express surprise, and
once more I asked him the way to the wonderful city. His hand
was steadier now and his eyes more intelligent, and he said
that he had heard something of some such city, but his memory was evidently blurred and he was still unable to give me
useful directions. I consequently gave him another tumbler,
which he drank off like the first without any water, and almost
at once he was a different man. The trembling in his hands
stopped altogether, his eye became as quick as a younger
man's, he answered my questions readily and frankly and,
what was more important to me still, his old memory became
alert and clear for even minutest details. His gratitude to
myself I need not mention, for I make no pretence that I
bought the bottle of whiskey that the old shepherd enjoyed so
much, without at least some thought of my own advantage. Yet
it was pleasant to reflect that it was due to me that he had
pulled himself together and steadied his shaking hand and
cleared his mind, recovered his memory and his self-respect.
He spoke to me quite clearly, no longer slurring his words; he
had seen the city first one moonlight night when he was lost in
the mist on the big moor; he had wandered far in the mist, and
when it lifted he saw the city by moonlight. He had no food, but
luckily had his flask. There was never such a city, not even in
books. Travellers talked sometimes of Venice seen from the
sea; there might be such a place or there might not, but,
whether or no, it was nothing to the city on Mallington Moor.
Men who read books had talked to him in his time, hundreds
of books, but they never could tell of any city like this. Why the
place was all of marble, roads, walls and palaces, all pure
white marble, and the tops of the tall thin spires were entirely
of gold. And they were queer folk in the city, even for foreign-

ers. And there were camels, but I cut him short, for I thought
I could judge for myself, if there was such a place, and, if not,
I was wasting my time as well as a pint of good whiskey. So I
got him to speak of the way, and after more circumlocution
than I needed and more talk of the city he pointed to a tiny
track on the black earth just beside us, a little twisty way you
could hardly see.

I said the moor was trackless; untrodden of man or dog it
certainly was and seemed to have less to do with the ways of
man than any waste I have seen, but the track the old shepherd showed me, if track it was, was no more than the track of
a hare—an elf-path the old man called it, Heaven knows what
he meant.

And then before I left him he insisted on giving me his flask
with the queer strong rum it contained. Whiskey brings out in
some men melancholy, in some rejoicing, with him it was clearly
generosity, and he insisted until I took his rum though I did not
mean to drink it. It was lonely up there, he said, and bitter cold,
and the city hard to find, being set in a hollow, and I should need
the rum, and he had never seen the marble city except on days
when he had had his flask. He seemed to regard that rusted iron
flask as a sort of mascot, and in the end I took it.

I followed that odd, faint track on the black earth under the
heather till I came to the big grey stone beyond the horizon
where the track divides into two, and I took the one to the left
as the old man told me. I knew by another stone that I saw far
off that I had not lost my way nor the old man lied.

And just as I hoped to see the city's ramparts before the
gloaming fell on that desolate place I suddenly saw a long high
wall of whiteness with pinnacles here and there thrown up
above it, floating towards me silent and grim as a secret, and
knew it for that evil thing the mist. The sun though low was
shining on every sprig of heather, the green and scarlet mosses
were shining with it too; it seemed incredible that in three
minutes' time all those colours would be gone and nothing left
all round but a grey darkness. I gave up hope of finding the
city that day, a broader path than mine could have been easily
lost. I hastily chose for my bed a thick patch of heather,
wrapped myself in a waterproof cloak, and lay down and made
myself comfortable. And then the mist came. It came like the
careful pulling of lace curtains, then like the drawing of grey
blinds; it shut out the horizon to the north, then to the east and

west; it turned the whole sky white and hid the moor; it came
down on it like a metropolis, only utterly silent, silent and
white as tombstones.

And then I was glad of that strange strong rum, or whatever
it was in the flask that the shepherd gave me: for I did not
think that the mist would clear till night, and I feared the
night would be cold. So I nearly emptied the flask; and sooner
than I expected I fell asleep, for the first night out as a rule one
does not sleep at once but is kept awake some while by the
little winds and the unfamiliar sound of the things that wander at night and that cry to one another far-off with their queer
faint voices; one misses them afterwards when one gets to
houses again. But I heard none of these sounds in the mist
that evening.

And then I woke and found that the mist was gone and the
sun was just disappearing under the moor, and I knew that I
had not slept for as long as I thought. And I decided to go on
while I could, for I thought that I was not very far from the
city.

I went on and on along the twisty track, bits of the mist
came down and filled the hollows but lifted again at once so
that I saw my way. The twilight faded as I went, a star
appeared, and I was able to see the track no longer. I could go
no further that night, yet before I lay down to sleep I decided
to go and look over the edge of a wide depression in the moor
that I saw a little way off. So I left the track and walked a few
hundred yards, and when I got to the edge the hollow was full
of mist all white underneath me. Another star appeared and a
cold wind arose, and with the wind the mist flapped away like
a curtain. And there was the city.

Nothing the shepherd had said was the least untrue or even
exaggerated. The poor old man had told the simple truth, there
is not a city like it in the world. What he had called thin spires
were minarets, but the little domes on the top were clearly
pure gold as he said. There were the marble terraces he
described, and the pure white palaces covered with carving,
and hundreds of minarets. The city was obviously of the East,
and yet where there should have been crescents on the domes
of the minarets there were golden suns with rays, and wherever one looked one saw things that obscured its origin. I
walked down to it and, passing through a wicket gate of gold
in a low wall of white marble, I entered the city. The heather

went right up to the city's edge and beat against the marble wall whenever the wind blew it. Lights began to twinkle from high windows of blue glass; as I walked up the white street, beautiful copper lanterns were lit up and let down from balconies by silver chains; from doors ajar came the sound of voices singing, and then I saw the men. Their faces were rather grey than black, and they wore beautiful robes of coloured silk with hems embroidered with gold and some with copper. And sometimes pacing down the marble ways with golden baskets hung on each side of them I saw the camels of which the old shepherd spoke.

The people had kindly faces, but though they were evidently friendly to strangers I could not speak with them being ignorant of their language, nor were the sounds of the syllables they used like any language I had ever heard, they sounded more like grouse.

When I tried to ask them by signs whence they had come with their city they would only point to the moon, which was bright and full and was shining fiercely on those marble ways till the city danced in light. And now there began appearing one by one, stepping softly out through windows, men with stringed instruments in the balconies. They were strange instruments with huge bulbs of wood and they played softly on them and very beautifully, and their queer voices softly sang to the music weird dirges of the griefs of their native land wherever that may be. And far off in the heart of the city others were singing too; the sound of it came to me wherever I roamed, not loud enough to disturb my thoughts but gently turning the mind to pleasant things. Slender carved arches of marble as delicate almost as lace crossed and re-crossed the ways wherever I went. There was none of that hurry of which foolish cities boast, nothing ugly or sordid so far as I could see. I saw that it was a city of beauty and song. I wondered how they had travelled with all that marble, how they had laid it down on Mallington Moor, whence they had come and what their resources were, and determined to investigate closely next morning, for the old shepherd had not troubled his head to think how the city came, he had only noted that the city was there (and of course no one believed him, though that is partly his fault for his dissolute ways). But at night one can see little and I had walked all day, so I determined to find a place to rest in. And just as I was wondering whether to ask for shelter of those silk-robed men by signs, or whether to sleep outside the walls and enter again in the morning, I came to a great archway in one of the marble houses with two black curtains, embroidered below with gold, hanging across it. Over the archway were carved apparently in many tongues the words: "Here strangers rest." In Greek, Latin and Spanish the sentence was repeated, and there was writing also in the language that you see on the walls of the great temples of Egypt, and Arabic, and what I took to be early Assyrian, and one or two languages I had never seen. I entered through the curtains, and found a tessellated marble court with golden braziers burning sleepy incense swinging by chains from the roof, all round the walls were comfortable mattresses lying upon the floor, covered with cloths and silks. It must have been ten o'clock and I was tired. Outside the music still softly filled the streets, a man had set a lantern down on the marble way, five or six sat down round him and he was sonorously telling them a story. Inside there were some already asleep on the beds; in the middle of the wide court under the braziers a woman dressed in blue was singing very gently; she did not move, but sung on and on, I never heard a song that was so soothing. I lay down on one of the mattresses by the wall, which was all inlaid with mosaics, and pulled over me some of the clothes with their beautiful alien work, and almost immediately my thoughts seemed part of the song that the woman was singing in the midst of the court under the golden braziers that hung from the high roof, and the song turned them to dreams and so I fell asleep.

A small wind having arisen I was awakened by a sprig of heather that beat continually against my face. It was morning on Mallington Moor and the city was quite gone.

Why the Milkman Shudders
When He Perceives the Dawn

In the Hall of the Ancient Company of Milkmen round the great fire-place at the end, when the winter logs are burning and all the craft are assembled, they tell to-day, as their grandfathers told before them, why the milkman shudders when he perceives the dawn.

When dawn comes creeping over the edges of hills, peers through the tree trunks making wonderful shadows, touches the tops of tall columns of smoke going up from awakening cottages in the valleys, and breaks all golden over Kentish fields, when going on tip-toe thence it comes to the walls of London and slips all shyly up those gloomy streets the milkman perceives it and shudders.

A man may be a Milkman's Working Apprentice, may know what borax is and how to mix it, yet not for that is the story told to him. There are five men alone that tell that story, five men appointed by the Master of the Company, by whom each place is filled as it falls vacant; and if you do not hear it from one of them you hear the story from none, and so can never know why the milkman shudders when he perceives the dawn.

It is the way of one of these five men, grey-beards all and milkmen from infancy, to rub his hands by the fire when the great logs burn, and to settle himself more easily in his chair, perhaps to sip some drink far other than milk, then to look round to see that none are there to whom it would not be fitting the tale should be told and, looking from face to face and seeing none but the men of the Ancient Company, and questioning mutely the rest of the five with his eyes, if some of the five be there, and receiving their permission, to cough and to tell the tale. And a great hush falls in the Hall of the Ancient Company, and something about the shape of the roof and the rafters makes the tale resonant all down the hall, so that the youngest hears it far away from the fire, and knows, and dreams of the day when perhaps he will tell himself, why the milkman shudders when he perceives the dawn.

Not as one tells some casual fact is it told, nor is it commented on from man to man, but is told by that great fire only and when the occasion and the stillness of the room and the merit of the wine and the profit of all seem to warrant it in the opinion of the five deputed men: then does one of them tell it, as I have said, not heralded by any master of ceremonies but as though it arose out of the warmth of the fire before which his knotted hands would chance to be; not a thing learned by rote, but told differently by each teller, and differently according to his mood, yet never has one of them dared to alter its salient points, there is none so base among the Company of Milkmen. The Company of Powderers for the Face know of this story and have envied it, the Worthy Company of Chin-Barbers, and the Company of Whiskerers; but none have heard it in the Milkmen's Hall, through whose wall no rumour of the secret goes, and though they have invented tales of their own Antiquity mocks them.

This mellow story was ripe with honourable years when milkmen wore beaver hats, its origin was still mysterious when white smocks were the vogue, men asked one another when Stuarts were on the throne (and only the Ancient Company knew the answer) why the milkman shudders when he perceives the dawn. It is all for envy of this tale's reputation that the Company of Powderers for the Face have invented the tale that they too tell of an evening "Why the Dog Barks when he hears the step of the Baker"; and because probably all men know that tale the Company of Powderers for the Face have dared to consider it famous. Yet it lacks mystery and is not ancient, is not fortified with classical allusion, has no secret lore, is common to all who care for an idle tale, and shares with "The Wars of the Elves," the Calf-butchers' tale, and "The Story of the Unicorn and the Rose," which is the tale of the Company of Horsedrivers, their obvious inferiority.

But unlike all these tales so new to time, and many another that the last two centuries tell, the tale that the milkman tell ripples wisely on, so full of quotation from the profoundest writers, so full of recondite allusion, so deeply tinged with all the wisdom of man and instructive with the experience of all times, that they that hear it in the Milkmen's Hall, as they interpret allusion after allusion and trace obscure quotation, lose idle curiosity and forget to question why the milkman shudders when he perceives the dawn.

You also, O my reader, give not yourself up to curiosity. Consider of how many it is the bane. Would you to gratify this tear away the mystery from the Milkmen's Hall and wrong the Ancient Company of Milkmen? Would they if all the world knew it and it became a common thing tell that tale any more that they have told for the last four hundred years? Rather a silence would settle upon their hall and a universal regret for the ancient tale and the ancient winter evenings. And though curiosity were a proper consideration yet even then this is not the proper place, nor this the proper occasion, for the tale. For the proper place is only the Milkmen's Hall, and the proper occasion only when logs burn well and when wine has been deeply drunken; then when the candles were burning well in long rows down to the dimness, down to the darkness and mystery that lie at the end of the hall, then were you one of the Company, and were I one of the five, would I rise from my seat by the fireside and tell you with all the embellishments that it has gleaned from the ages that story that is the heirloom of the milkmen. And the long candles would burn lower and lower, and gutter and gutter away, till they liquefied in their sockets, and draughts would blow from the shadowy end of the hall stronger and stronger till the shadows came after them, and still I would hold you with that treasured story, not by any wit of mine but all for the sake of its glamour and the times out of which it came; one by one the candles would flare and die and, when all were gone, by the light of ominous sparks, when each milkman's face looks fearful to his fellow, you would know, as now you cannot, why the milkman shudders when he perceives the dawn.

The Bad Old Woman in Black

The bad old woman in black ran down the street of the ox-butchers.

Windows at once were opened high up in those crazy gables; heads were thrust out: it was she. Then there arose the counsel of anxious voices, calling sideways from window to window or across to opposite houses. Why was she there with her sequins and bugles and old black gown? Why had she left her dreaded house? On what fell errand she hasted?

They watched her lean lithe figure and the wind in that old black dress, and soon she was gone from the cobbled street and under the town's high gateway. She turned at once to her right and was hid from the view of the houses. Then they all ran down to their doors, and small groups formed on the pavement, there they took counsel together, the eldest speaking first. Of what they had seen they said nothing for there was no doubt it was she, it was of the future they spoke and the future only.

In what notorious thing would her errand end? What gains had tempted her out from her fearful home? What brilliant but sinful scheme had her genius planned? Above all what future evil did this portend? Thus at first it was only questions. And then the old grey-beards spoke, each one to a little group; they had seen her out before, had known her when she was young, and had noted the evil things that had followed her goings: the small groups listened well to their low and earnest voices. No one asked questions now or guessed at her infamous errand, but listened only to the wise old men who knew the things that had been and who told the younger men of the dooms that had come before.

Nobody knew how many times she had left her dreaded house, but the oldest recounted all the times that they knew, and the way she had gone each time, and the doom that had followed her going; and two could remember the earthquake that there was in the street of the shearers.

So were there many tales of the times that were, told on the pavement near the old green doors by the edge of the cobbled street, and the experience that the aged men had bought with their white hairs might be had cheap by the young. But from all their experience only this was clear, that never twice in their lives had she done the same infamous thing, and that the same calamity twice had never followed her doings. Therefore it seemed that means were doubtful and few for finding out what thing was about to befall, and an ominous feeling of gloom came down on the street of the ox-butchers. And in the gloom grew fears of the very worst. This comfort they only had when they put their fears into words—that the doom that followed her doings had never yet been anticipated. One feared that with magic she meant to move the moon, and he would have dammed the high tide on the neighbouring coast, knowing that as the moon attracted the sea the sea must attract the moon, and hoping by his device to humble her spells. Another would have fetched iron bars and clamped them across the street, remembering the earthquake there was in the street of the shearers. Another would have honoured his household gods, the little cat-faced idols seated above his hearth, gods to whom magic was no unusual thing, and having paid their fees and honoured them well would have put the whole case before them. His scheme found favour with many, and yet at last was rejected, for others ran indoors and brought out their gods too to be honoured, till there were a herd of gods all seated there on the pavement; yet would they have honoured them and put their case before them but that a fat man ran up last of all, carefully holding under a reverent arm his own two hound-faced gods, though he knew well, as indeed all men must, that they were notoriously at war with the little cat-faced idols. And although the animosities natural to faith had all been lulled by the crisis, yet a look of anger had come in the cat-like faces that no one dared disregard, and all perceived that if they stayed a moment longer there would be flaming around them the jealousy of the gods; so each man hastily took his idols home, leaving the fat man insisting that his hound-faced gods should be honoured.

Then were there schemes again and voices raised in debate, and many new dangers feared and new plans made.

But in the end they made no defence against danger, for they knew not what it would be, but wrote upon parchment as a warning and in order that all might know: *"The bad old woman in black ran down the street of the ox-butchers."*

The Bird of
the Difficult Eye

Observant men and women that know their Bond Street
well will appreciate my astonishment when in a jeweller's
shop I perceived that nobody was furtively watching me. Not
only this, but when I even picked up a little carved crystal to
examine it no shop-assistants crowded round me. I walked the
whole length of the shop, still no one politely followed.

Seeing from this that some extraordinary revolution had
occurred in the jewelry business, I went with my curiosity well
aroused to a queer old person, half demon and half man, who
has an idol-shop in a by-way of the City and who keeps me
informed of affairs of the Edge of the World. And briefly over a
pinch of heathen incense, that he takes by way of snuff, he
gave me this tremendous information: that Mr. Neepy Thang,
the son of Thangobrind, had returned from the Edge of the
World and was even now in London.

The information may not appear tremendous to those unacquainted with the source of jewelry; but when I say that the only
thief employed by any West-end jeweller since famous
Thangobrind's distressing doom is this same Neepy Thang,
and that for lightness of fingers and swiftness of stockinged foot they
have none better in Paris, it will be understood why the Bond
Street jewellers no longer cared what became of their old stock.

There were big diamonds in London that summer and a few
considerable sapphires. In certain astounding kingdoms
behind the East strange sovereigns missed from their turbans
the heirlooms of ancient wars, and here and there the keepers
of crown jewels, who had not heard the stockinged feet of
Thang, were questioned and died slowly.

And the jewellers gave a little dinner to Thang at the Hôtel
Great Magnificent; the windows had not been opened for five
years, and there was wine at a guinea a bottle that you could
not tell from champagne, and cigars at half a crown with a
Havana label. Altogether it was a splendid evening for Thang.

84

But I have to tell of a far sadder thing than a dinner at an hotel. The public require jewelry, and jewelry must be obtained. I have to tell of Neepy Thang's last journey. That year the fashion was emeralds. A man named Green had recently crossed the Channel on a bicycle and the jewellers said that a green stone would be particularly appropriate to commemorate the event, and recommended emeralds.

Now a certain moneylender of Cheapside who had just been made a peer had divided his gains into three equal parts: one for the purchase of the peerage, country-house and park, and the twenty thousand pheasants that are absolutely essential, and one for the upkeep of the position; while the third he banked abroad, partly to cheat the native tax-gatherer, and partly because it seemed to him that the days of the Peerage were few and that he might at any moment be called upon to start afresh elsewhere. In the upkeep of the position he included jewelry for his wife, and so it came about that Lord Castlenorman placed an order with two well-known Bond Street Jews named Messrs. Grosvenor and Campbell to the extent of £100,000 for a few reliable emeralds.

But the emeralds in stock were mostly small and shop-soiled, and Neepy Thang had to set out at once before he had had as much as a week in London. I will briefly sketch his project. Not many knew it, for where the form of business is black-mail the fewer creditors you have the better (which of course in various degrees applies at all times).

On the shores of the risky seas of Shiroora Shan grows one tree only, so that upon its branches if anywhere in the world there must build its nest the Bird of the Difficult Eye. Neepy Thang had come by this information, which was indeed the truth, that if the bird migrated to Fairyland before the three eggs hatched out they would undoubtedly all turn into emer-alds, while if they hatched out first it would be a bad business.

When he had mentioned these eggs to Messrs. Grosvenor and Campbell they had said "The very thing": they were men of few words, in English, for it was not their native tongue.

So Neepy Thang set out. He bought the purple ticket at Victoria Station. He went by Herne Hill, Bromley and Bickley and passed St. Mary Cray. At Eynsford he changed, and taking a footpath along a winding valley went wandering into the hills. And at the top of a hill in a little wood, where all the anemones long since were over, and the perfume of mint and thyme from outside came drifting in with Thang, he found once more the familiar path, age-old and fair as wonder, that leads to the Edge of the World. Little to him were its sacred memories that are one with the secret of earth, for he was out on business, and little would they be to me if I ever put them on paper. Let it suffice that he went down that path going further and further from the fields we know, and all the way he muttered to himself, "What if the eggs hatch out and it be a bad business!" The glamour that is at all times upon those lonely lands that lie at the back of the chalky hills of Kent intensified as he went upon his journeys. Queerer and queerer grew the things that he saw by little World-End Path. Many a twilight descended upon that journey with all their mysteries, many a blaze of stars; many a morning came flaming up to a tinkle of silvern horns; till the outpost elves of Fairyland came in sight, and the glittering crests of Fairyland's three mountains betokened the journey's end. And so with painful steps (for the shores of the World are covered with huge crystals) he came to the risky seas of Shiroora Shan and saw them pounding to gravel the wreckage of fallen stars, saw them and heard their roar, those shipless seas that between earth and the fairies' homes heave beneath some huge wind that is none of our four. And there in the darkness on the grizzly coast, for darkness was swooping slantwise down the sky as though with some evil purpose, there stood that lonely, gnarled and deciduous tree. It was a bad place to be found in after dark, and night descended with multitudes of stars, beasts prowling in the blackness gluttered* at Neepy Thang. And there on a lower branch within easy reach he clearly saw the Bird of the Difficult Eye sitting upon the nest for which she is famous. Her face was towards those three inscrutable mountains, far-off on the other side of the risky seas, whose hidden valleys are fairyland. Though not yet autumn in the fields we know, it was close on mid-winter here, the moment as Thang knew well when those eggs hatch out. Had he miscalculated and arrived a minute too late? Yet the bird was even now about to migrate, her pinions fluttered and her gaze was toward fairyland. Thang hoped, and muttered a prayer to those pagan gods whose spite and vengeance he had most reason to fear. It seems that it was too

---

*See any dictionary, but in vain.

late or a prayer too small to placate them, for there and then
the stroke of mid-winter came and the eggs hatched out in the
roar of Shiroora Shan or ever the bird was gone with her difficult eye, and it was a bad business indeed for Neepy Thang; I
haven't the heart to tell you any more.

"'Ere," said Lord Castlenorman some few weeks later to
Messrs. Grosvenor and Campbell, "you aren't 'arf taking your
time about those emeralds."

The Long Porter's Tale

There are things that are only known to the long porter of Tong Tong Tarrup as he sits and mumbles memories to himself in the little bastion gateway.

He remembers the war there was in the halls of the gnomes, and how the fairies came for the opals once which Tong Tong Tarrup has, the way that the giants went through the fields, below, he watching from his gateway, he remembers quests that are even yet a wonder to the gods. Who dwells in those frozen houses on the high, bare brink of the world not even he has told me, and he is held to be garrulous. Among the elves, the only living thing ever seen moving at that awful altitude where they quarry turquoise on Earth's highest crag, his name is a byword for loquacity wherewith they mock the talkative.

His favourite story if you offer him bash, the drug of which he is fondest and for which he will give his service in war to the elves against the goblins or vice versa if the goblins bring him more, his favourite story when bodily soothed by the drug and mentally fiercely excited tells of a quest undertaken ever so long ago for nothing more marketable than an old woman's song.

Picture him telling it. An old man lean and bearded and almost monstrously long that lolled in a city's gateway on a crag perhaps ten miles high; the houses for the most part facing earthward, lit by the sun and moon and the constellations we know, but one house on the pinnacle looking over the edge of the world and lit by the glimmer of those unearthly spaces where one long evening wears away the stars; never a street in the city, only a multitude of wayward stairs; my little offering of bash: a long forefinger that nipped it at once on a stained and greedy thumb: all these are in the foreground of the picture. In the background, the mystery of those silent houses and of not knowing who their denizens were, or what service they had at the hands of the long porter and what payment he had in return and whether he was mortal.

Picture him in the gateway of this incredible town, having

swallowed my bash in silence, stretch his great length, lean back and begin to speak.

It seems that one clear morning a hundred years ago a visitor to Tong Tong Tarrup was climbing up from the world. He had already passed above the snow, and had set his foot on a step of the earthward stairway that goes down from Tong Tong Tarrup on to the rocks, when the long porter saw him. And so painfully did he climb those easy steps that the grizzled man on watch had long to wonder whether or not the stranger brought him bash, the drug that gives a meaning to the stars and seems to explain the twilight. And in the end there was not a scrap of bash, and the stranger had nothing better to offer that grizzled man than his mere story only.

It seems that the stranger's name was Gerald Jones, and he always lived in London, but once as a child he had been on a Northern moor; it was so long ago that he did not remember how, only somehow or other he walked alone on the moor and all the ling was in flower. There was nothing in sight but ling and heather and bracken except that far off near the sunset on indistinct hills there were little vague patches that looked like the fields of men. With evening a mist crept up and hid the hills, and still he went walking on over the moor. And then he came on the valley, a tiny valley in the midst of the moor, whose sides were incredibly steep. He lay down and looked at it through the roots of the ling. And a long, long way below him, in a garden by a cottage, with hollyhocks all round her that were taller than herself, there sat an old woman on a wooden chair, singing in the evening. And the man had taken a fancy to the song and remembered it after in London, and whenever it came to his mind it made him think of evenings—the kind you don't get in London—and he heard a soft wind again going idly over the moor, and the bumblebees in a hurry, and forgot the noise of the traffic. And always whenever he heard men speak of Time, he grudged to Time most this song. Once afterwards he went to that Northern moor again and found the tiny valley, but there was no old woman in the garden and no one was singing a song. And either regret for the song that the old woman had sung, on a summer evening twenty years away and daily receding, troubled his mind, or else the wearisome work that he did in London, for he worked for a great firm that was perfectly useless; and he grew old early as men do in cities. And at last when melancholy brought only regret and the uselessness of his work gained ground with age, he decided to consult a magician. So to a magician he went and told him his troubles, and particularly he told him how he had heard the song, "and now," he said, "it is nowhere in the world."

"Of course it is not in the world," the magician said, "but over the Edge of the World you may easily find it." And he told the man that he was suffering from flux of Time, and recommended a day at the Edge of the World. Jones asked what part of the Edge of the World he should go to, and the magician had heard of Tong Tong Tarrup well spoken of, so Jones paid him as is usual in opals and started at once on the journey. The ways to that town are winding: he took the ticket at Victoria Station that they only give if they know you: he went past Bleth: he went along the hills of Neol-Hungar and came to the Gap of Poy. All these are in that part of the world that pertains to the fields we know, but beyond the Gap of Poy on those ordinary plains that so closely resemble Sussex one first meets the unlikely. A line of common grey hills, the Hills of Sneg, may be seen at the edge of the plain from the Gap of Poy, it is there that the incredible begins, infrequently at first but happening more and more as you go up the hills. For instance, descending once into Poy Plains, the first thing that I saw was an ordinary shepherd watching a flock of ordinary sheep. I looked at them for some time and nothing happened, when without a word one of the sheep walked up to the shepherd and borrowed his pipe and smoked it, an incident that struck me as unlikely; but in the Hills of Sneg I met an honest politician. Over these plains went Jones and over the Hills of Sneg, meeting at first unlikely things and then incredible things, till he came to the long slope beyond the hills that leads up to the Edge of the World and where, as all guide-books tell, anything may happen. You might at the foot of this slope see here and there things that could conceivably occur in the fields we know, but soon these disappeared and the traveller saw nothing but fabulous beasts, browsing on flowers as astounding as themselves, and rocks so distorted that their shapes had clearly a meaning, being too startling to be accidental. Even the trees were shockingly unfamiliar, they had so much to say, and they leant over to one another whenever they spoke and struck grotesque attitudes and leered. Jones saw two fir-trees fighting. The effect of these scenes on his nerves was very severe, still he climbed on and was much cheered at last by the sight of a primrose, the only familiar thing he had seen for hours—but it whistled and skipped away. He saw the unicorns in their secret valley. Then night in a sinister way slipped over the sky and there shone not only the stars but lesser and greater moons, and he heard dragons rattling in the dark.

With dawn there appeared above him among its amazing crags the town of Tong Tong Tarrup with the light on its frozen stairs, a tiny cluster of houses far up in the sky. He was on steep mountain now; great mists were leaving it slowly and revealing, as they trailed away, more and more astonishing things. Before the mist had all gone he heard quite near him, on what he had thought was bare mountain, the sound of a heavy galloping on turf. He had come to the plateau of the centaurs. And all at once he saw them in the mist: there they were, the children of fable, five enormous centaurs. Had he paused on account of any astonishment he had not come so far; he strode on over the plateau and came quite near to the centaurs. It is never the centaurs' wont to notice men; they pawed the ground and shouted to one another in Greek, but they said no word to him. Nevertheless they turned and stared at him when he left them, and when he had crossed the plateau and still went on all five of them cantered after to the edge of their green land; for above the high green plateau of the centaurs is nothing but naked mountain, and the last green thing that is seen by the mountaineer as he travels to Tong Tong Tarrup is the grass that the centaurs trample. He came into the snow fields that the mountain wears like a cape, its head being bare above it, and still climbed on. The centaurs watched him with increasing wonder.

Not even fabulous beasts were near him now nor strange demoniac trees, nothing but snow and the clean bare crag above it on which was Tong Tong Tarrup. All day he climbed and evening found him above the snow-line, and soon he came to the stairway cut in the rock and in sight of that grizzled man, the long porter of Tong Tong Tarrup, sitting mumbling amazing memories to himself and expecting in vain from the stranger a gift of bash.

It seems that as soon as the stranger arrived at the bastion gateway, tired though he was he demanded lodgings at once that commanded a good view of the Edge of the World. But the long porter, that grizzled man, disappointed of his bash, demanded the stranger's story to add to his memories before he would show him the way. And this is the story if the long porter has told me the truth and if his memory is still what it was. And when the story was told that grizzled man arose and dangling his musical keys, went up through door after door and by many stairs and led the stranger to the topmost house, the highest roof in the world, and in its parlour showed him the parlour window. There the tired stranger sat down in a chair and gazed out of the window sheer over the Edge of the World. The window was shut and in its glittering panes the twilight of World's Edge blazed and danced, partly like glow-worms' lamps and partly like the sea it went by rippling, full of wonderful moons. But the traveller did not look at the wonderful moons. For from the abyss there grew with their roots in far constellations a row of hollyhocks, and amongst them a small green garden quivered and trembled as scenes tremble in water; higher up ling in bloom was floating upon the twilight; more and more floated up till all the twilight was purple, the little green garden low down was hung in the midst of it. And the garden down below and the ling all round it seemed all to be trembling and drifting on a song. For the twilight was full of a song that sang and rang along the edges of the World, and the green garden and the ling seemed to flicker and ripple with it as the song rose and fell, and an old woman was singing it down in the garden. A bumble-bee sailed across from over the Edge of the World. And the song that was lapping there against the coasts of the World and to which the stars were dancing was the same that he had heard the old woman sing long since down in the valley in the midst of the Northern moor.

But that grizzled man, the long porter, would not let the stranger stay, because he brought him no bash; and impatiently he shouldered him away, himself not troubling to glance through the World's outermost window, for the lands that Time afflicts and the spaces that Time knows not are all one to that grizzled man, and the bash that he eats more profoundly astounds his mind than anything man can show him either in the World we know or over the Edge. And bitterly protesting the traveller went back and down again to the World.

· · · · ·

Accustomed as I am to the incredible from knowing the Edge of the World the story presents difficulties to me. Yet it may be that the devastation wrought by Time is merely local and that outside the scope of his destruction old songs are still being sung by those that we deem dead. I try to hope so. And yet the more I investigate the story that the long porter told me in the town of Tong Tong Tarrup the more plausible the alternative theory appears—that that grizzled man is a liar.

The Bureau d'Echange de Maux

I often think of the Bureau d'Echange de Maux and the won-
drously evil old man that sate therein. It stood in a little
street that there is in Paris, its doorway made of three brown
beams of wood, the top one overlapping the others like the
Greek letter pai, all the rest painted green, a house far lower
and narrower than its neighbours and infinitely stranger, a
thing to take one's fancy. And over the doorway on the old
brown beam in faded yellow letters this legend ran, "Bureau
Universel d'Echange de Maux."

I entered at once and accosted the listless man that lolled on
a stool by his counter. I demanded the wherefore of his wonderful house, what evil wares he exchanged, with many other
things that I wished to know, for curiosity led me: and indeed
had it not I had gone at once from the shop, for there was so evil
a look in that fattened man, in the hang of his fallen cheeks and
his sinful eye, that you would have said he had had dealings
with Hell and won the advantage by sheer wickedness.

Such a man was mine host, but above all the evil of him lay
in his eyes, which lay so still, so apathetic, that you would have
sworn that he was drugged or dead; like lizards motionless on
a wall they lay, then suddenly they darted, and all his cunning
flamed up and revealed itself in what one moment before
seemed no more than a sleepy and ordinary wicked old man.
And this was the object and trade of that peculiar shop, the
Bureau Universel d'Echange de Maux: you paid twenty francs,
which the old man proceeded to take from me, for admission to
the bureau, and then had the right to exchange any evil or mis-
fortune with anyone on the premises for some evil or misfor-
tune that he "could afford," as the old man put it.

There were four or five men in the dingy ends of that low-
ceilinged room who gesticulated and muttered softly in twos as
men who make a bargain, and now and then more came in,
and the eyes of the flabby owner of the house leaped up at
them as they entered, seemed to know their errands at once

and each one's peculiar need, and fell back again into somno-
lence, receiving his twenty francs in an almost lifeless hand
and biting the coin as though in pure absence of mind.

"Some of my clients," he told me. So amazing to me was the
trade of this extraordinary shop that I engaged the old man in
conversation, repulsive though he was, and from his garrulity I
gathered these facts. He spoke in perfect English though his
utterance was somewhat thick and heavy, no language seemed to
come amiss to him. He had been in business a great many years,
how many he would not say, and was far older than he looked. All
kinds of people did business in his shop. What they exchanged
with each other he did not care, except that it had to be evils; he
was not empowered to carry on any other kind of business.

There was no evil, he told me, that was not negotiable there; no
evil the old man knew had ever been taken away in despair from
his shop. A man might have to wait and come back again next day
and next day and the day after, paying twenty francs each time,
but the old man had the addresses of his clients and shrewdly
knew their needs, and soon the right two met and eagerly
changed their commodities. "Commodities" was the old man's terrible word, said with a gruesome smack of his heavy lips, for he
took a pride in his business and evils to him were goods.

I learned from him in ten minutes very much of human
nature, more than I had ever learned from any other man; I
learned from him that a man's own evil is to him the worst
thing that there is or could be, and that an evil so unbalances
all men's minds that they always seek for extremes in that
small grim shop. A woman that had no children had exchanged
with an impoverished half-maddened creature with twelve. On
one occasion a man had exchanged wisdom for folly.

"Why on earth did he do that?" I said.

"None of my business," the old man answered in his heavy
indolent way. He merely took his twenty francs from each and
ratified the agreement in the little room at the back opening
out of the shop where his clients do business. Apparently the
man that had parted with wisdom had left the shop upon the
tips of his toes with a happy though foolish expression all over
his face, but the other went thoughtfully away wearing a troubled and very puzzled look. Almost always it seemed they did
business in opposite evils.

But the thing that puzzled me most in all my talks with that
unwieldy man, the thing that puzzles me still, is that none that

had once done business in that shop ever returned again; a man might come day after day for many weeks, but once do business and he never returned; so much the old man told me, but, when I asked him why, he only muttered that he did not know.

It was to discover the wherefore of this strange thing, and for no other reason at all, that I determined myself to do business sooner or later in the little room at the back of that mysterious shop. I determined to exchange some very trivial evil for some evil equally slight, to seek for myself an advantage so very small as scarcely to give Fate as it were a grip; for I deeply distrusted these bargains, knowing well that man has never yet benefited by the marvellous and that the more miraculous his advantage appears to be the more securely and tightly do the gods or the witches catch him. In a few days more I was going back to England and I was beginning to fear that I should be sea-sick: this fear of sea-sickness, not the actual malady but only the mere fear of it, I decided to exchange for a suitably little evil. I did not know with whom I should be dealing, who in reality was the head of the firm (one never does when shopping), but I decided that neither Jew nor Devil could make very much on so small a bargain as that.

I told the old man my project, and he scoffed at the smallness of my commodity, trying to urge me on to some darker bargain, but could not move me from my purpose. And then he told me tales with a somewhat boastful air of the big business, the great bargains, that had passed through his hands. A man had once run in there to try and exchange death; he had swallowed poison by accident and had only twelve hours to live. That sinister old man had been able to oblige him. A client was willing to exchange the commodity.

"But what did he give in exchange for death?" I said.

"Life," said that grim old man with a furtive chuckle.

"It must have been a horrible life," I said.

"That was not my affair," the proprietor said, lazily rattling together as he spoke a little pocketful of twenty-franc pieces.

Strange business I watched in that shop for the next few days, the exchange of odd commodities, and heard strange mutterings in corners amongst couples who presently rose and went to the back room, the old man following to ratify.

Twice a day for a week I paid my twenty francs, watching life with its great needs and its little needs morning and afternoon spread out before me in all its wonderful variety.

And one day I met a comfortable man with only a little need, he seemed to have the very evil I wanted. He always feared the lift was going to break. I knew too much of hydraulics to fear things as silly as that, but it was not my business to cure his ridiculous fear. Very few words were needed to convince him that mine was the evil for him, he never crossed the sea, and I, on the other hand, could always walk upstairs, and I also felt at the time, as many must feel in that shop, that so absurd a fear could never trouble me. And yet at times it is almost the curse of my life. When we both had signed the parchment in the spidery back room and the old man had signed and ratified (for which we had to pay him fifty francs each) I went back to my hotel, and there I saw the deadly thing in the basement. They asked me if I would go upstairs in the lift; from force of habit I risked it, and I held my breath all the way up and clenched my hands. Nothing will induce me to try such a journey again. I would sooner go up to my room in a balloon. And why? Because if a balloon goes wrong you have a chance, it may spread out into a parachute after it has burst, it may catch in a tree, a hundred and one things may happen, but if the lift falls down its shaft you are done. As for sea-sickness I shall never be sick again, I cannot tell you why except that I know that it is so.

And the shop in which I made this remarkable bargain, the shop to which none return when their business is done: I set out for it next day. Blindfold I could have found my way to the unfashionable quarter out of which a mean street runs, where you take the alley at the end, whence runs the cul-de-sac where the queer shop stood. A shop with pillars, fluted and painted red, stands on its near side, its other neighbour is a low-class jeweller's with little silver brooches in the window. In such incongruous company stood the shop with beams, with its walls painted green.

In half an hour I stood in the cul-de-sac to which I had gone twice a day for the last week. I found the shop with the ugly painted pillars and the jeweller that sold brooches, but the green house with the tree beams was gone.

Pulled down, you will say, although in a single night. That can never be the answer to the mystery, for the house of the fluted pillars painted on plaster, and the low-class jeweller's shop with its silver brooches (all of which I could identify one by one) were standing side by side.

A Story of Land and Sea

It is written in the first Book of Wonder how Captain Shard of the bad ship *Desperate Lark,* having looted the sea-coast city Bombasharna, retired from active life; and resigning piracy to younger men, with the goodwill of the North and South Atlantic, settled down with a captured queen on his floating island.

Sometimes he sank a ship for the sake of old times, but he no longer hovered along the trade-routes; and timid merchants watched for other men.

It was not age that caused him to leave his romantic profession; nor unworthiness of its traditions, nor gunshot wound, nor drink; but grim necessity and *force majeure.* Five navies were after him. How he gave them the slip one day in the Mediterranean, how he fought with the Arabs, how a ship's broadside was heard in Lat. 23 N. Long. 4 E. for the first time and the last, with other things unknown to Admiralties, I shall proceed to tell.

He had had his fling, had Shard, captain of pirates, and all his merry men wore pearls in their ear-rings; and now the English fleet was after him under full sail along the coast of Spain with a good north wind behind them. They were not gaining much on Shard's rakish craft, the bad ship *Desperate Lark,* yet they were closer than was to his liking, and they interfered with business.

For a day and a night they had chased him, when off Cape Vincent at about 6 A.M. Shard took that step that decided his retirement from active life, he turned for the Mediterranean. Had he held on southwards down the African coast it is doubtful whether in face of the interference of England, Russia, France, Denmark and Spain, he could have made piracy pay; but in turning for the Mediterranean he took what we may call the penultimate step of his life which meant for him settling down. There were three great courses of action invented by Shard in his youth, upon which he pondered by day and

97

brooded by night, consolations in all his dangers, secret even from his men, three means of escape as he hoped from any peril that might meet him on the sea. One of these was the floating island that the Book of Wonder tells of, another was so fantastic that we may doubt if even the brilliant audacity of Shard could ever have found it practicable, at least he never tried it so far as is known in that tavern by the sea in which I glean my news, and the third he determined on carrying out as he turned that morning for the Mediterranean. True, he might yet have practised piracy in spite of the step that he took, a little later when the seas grew quiet, but that penultimate step was like that small house in the country that the business man has his eye on; like some snug investment put away for old age, there are certain final courses in men's lives which after taking they never go back to business.

He turned then for the Mediterranean with the English fleet behind him, and his men wondered.

What madness was this—muttered Bill, the boatswain, in Old Frank's only ear—with the French fleet waiting in the Gulf of Lyons and the Spaniards all the way between Sardinia and Tunis: for they knew the Spaniards' ways. And they made a deputation and waited upon Captain Shard, all of them sober and wearing their costly clothes; and they said that the Mediterranean was a trap, and all he said was that the north wind should hold. And the crew said they were done.

So they entered the Mediterranean, and the English Fleet came up and closed the straits. And Shard went tacking along the Moroccan coast with a dozen frigates behind him. And the north wind grew in strength. And not till evening did he speak to his crew, and then he gathered them all together except the man at the helm, and politely asked them to come down to the hold. And there he showed them six immense steel axles and a dozen low iron wheels of enormous width which none had seen before; and he told his crew how all unknown to the world his keel had been specially fitted for these same axles and wheels, and how he meant soon to sail to the wide Atlantic again, though not by the way of the straits. And when they heard the name of the Atlantic all his merry men cheered, for they looked on the Atlantic as a wide safe sea.

And night came down and Captain Shard sent for his diver. With the sea getting up it was hard work for the diver, but by midnight things were done to Shard's satisfaction; and the diver said that of all the jobs he had done, . . . but finding no apt comparison, and being in need of a drink, silence fell on him and soon sleep, and his comrades carried him away to his hammock. All the next day the chase went on with the English well in sight, for Shard had lost time overnight with his wheels and axles, and the danger of meeting the Spaniards increased every hour; and evening came when every minute seemed dangerous, yet they still went tacking on towards the East where they knew the Spaniards must be.

And at last they sighted their topsails right ahead, and still Shard went on. It was a close thing, but night was coming on, and the Union Jack which he hoisted helped Shard with the Spaniards for the last few anxious minutes, though it seemed to anger the English, but as Shard said, "There's no pleasing everyone," and then the twilight shivered into darkness.

"Hard to starboard," said Captain Shard.

The north wind which had risen all day was now blowing a gale. I do not know what part of the coast Shard steered for, but Shard knew, for the coasts of the world were to him what Margate is to some of us.

At a place where the desert rolling up from mystery and from death, yea from the heart of Africa, emerges upon the sea, no less grand than her, no less terrible, even there they sighted the land quite close, almost in darkness. Shard ordered every man to the hinder part of the ship and all the ballast too; and soon the *Desperate Lark,* her prow a little high out of the water, doing her eighteen knots before the wind, struck a sandy beach and shuddered; she heeled over a little, then righted herself, and slowly headed into the interior of Africa.

The men would have given three cheers, but after the first Shard silenced them and, steering the ship himself, he made them a short speech while the broad wheels pounded slowly over the African sand, doing barely five knots in a gale. The perils of the sea, he said, had been greatly exaggerated. Ships had been sailing the sea for hundreds of years, and at sea you knew what to do, but on land this was different. They were on land now and they were not to forget it. At sea you might make as much noise as you pleased and no harm was done, but on land anything might happen. One of the perils of the land that he instanced was that of hanging. For every hundred men that they hung on land, he said, not more than twenty would be hung at sea. The men were to sleep at their guns. They would not go far that night; for the risk of being wrecked at night was another danger peculiar to the land, while at sea you might sail from set of sun till dawn: yet it was essential to get out of sight of the sea, for if anyone knew they were there they'd have cavalry after them. And he had sent back Smerdrak (a young lieutenant of pirates) to cover their tracks where they came up from the sea. And the merry men vigorously nodded their heads though they did not dare to cheer, and presently Smerdrak came running up and they threw him a rope by the stern. And when they had done fifteen knots they anchored, and Captain Shard gathered his men about him and, standing by the land-wheel in the bows, under the large and clear Algerian stars, he explained his system of steering. There was not much to be said for it; he had with considerable ingenuity detached and pivoted the portion of the keel that held the leading axle and could move it by chains which were controlled from the land-wheel, thus the front pair of wheels could be deflected at will, but only very slightly, and they afterwards found that in a hundred yards they could only turn their ship four yards from her course. But let not captains of comfortable battleships, or owners even of yachts, criticize too harshly a man who was not of their time and who knew not modern contrivances; it should be remembered also that Shard was no longer at sea. His steering may have been clumsy but he did what he could.

When the use and limitations of his land-wheel had been made clear to his men, Shard bade them all turn in except those on watch. Long before dawn he woke them and by the very first gleam of light they got their ship under way, so that when those two fleets that had made so sure of Shard closed in like a great crescent on the Algerian coast there was no sign to see of the *Desperate Lark* either on sea or land; and the flags of the Admiral's ship broke out into a hearty English oath.

The gale blew for three days and, Shard using more sail by daylight, they scudded over the sands at little less than ten knots, though on the report of rough water ahead (as the lookout man called rocks, low hills or uneven surface before he adapted himself to his new surroundings) the rate was much decreased. Those were long summer days and Shard, who was anxious while the wind held good to outpace the rumour of his own appearance, sailed for nineteen hours a day, lying to at ten in the evening and hoisting sail again at 3 A.M., when it first began to be light.

In those three days he did five hundred miles; then the wind dropped to a breeze, though it still blew from the north, and for a week they did no more than two knots an hour. The merry men began to murmur then. Luck had distinctly favoured Shard at first, for it sent him at ten knots through the only populous districts well ahead of crowds except those who chose to run, and the cavalry were away on a local raid. As for the runners they soon dropped off when Shard pointed his cannon though he did not dare to fire, up there near the coast; for much as he jeered at the intelligence of the English and Spanish Admirals in not suspecting his manœuvre, the only one as he said that was possible in the circumstances, yet he knew that cannon had an obvious sound which would give his secret away to the weakest mind. Certainly luck had befriended him, and when it did so no longer he made out of the occasion all that could be made; for instance, while the wind held good he had never missed opportunities to revictual; if he passed by a village its pigs and poultry were his, and whenever he passed by water he filled his tanks to the brim, and now that he could only do two knots he sailed all night with a man and a lantern before him: thus in that week he did close on four hundred miles while another man would have anchored at night and have missed five or six hours out of the twenty-four. Yet his men murmured. Did he think the wind would last for ever, they said. And Shard only smoked. It was clear that he was thinking, and thinking hard. "But what is he thinking about?" said Bill to Bad Jack. And Bad Jack answered: "He may think as hard as he likes, but thinking won't get us out of the Sahara if this wind were to drop."

And towards the end of that week Shard went to his chart-room and laid a new course for his ship a little to the east and towards cultivation. And one day towards evening they sighted a village, and twilight came and the wind dropped altogether. Then the murmurs of the merry men grew to oaths and nearly to mutiny. "Where were they now?" they asked, and were they being treated like poor honest men?

Shard quieted them by asking what they wished to do themselves, and when no one had any better plan than going to the villagers and saying that they had been blown out of their course by a storm, Shard unfolded his scheme to them.

Long ago he had heard how they drove carts with oxen in Africa; oxen were very numerous in these parts wherever there was any cultivation, and for this reason when the wind had begun to drop he had laid his course for the village: that night the moment it was dark they were to drive off fifty yoke of oxen; by midnight they must all be yoked to the bows and then away they would go at a good round gallop.

So fine a plan as this astonished the men and they all apologized for their want of faith in Shard, shaking hands with him every one, and spitting on their hands before they did so in token of goodwill.

The raid that night succeeded admirably; but ingenious as Shard was on land, and a past-master at sea, yet it must be admitted that lack of experience in this class of seamanship led him to make a mistake, a slight one it is true, and one that a little practice would have prevented altogether: the oxen could not gallop. Shard swore at them, threatened them with his pistol, said they should have no food, and all to no avail: that night and as long as they pulled the bad ship *Desperate Lark* they did one knot an hour and no more. Shard's failures like everything that came his way were used as stones in the edifice of his future success, he went at once to his chart-room and worked out all his calculations anew.

The matter of the oxen's pace made pursuit impossible to avoid. Shard therefore countermanded his order to his lieutenant to cover the tracks in the sand, and the *Desperate Lark* plodded on into the Sahara on her new course trusting to her guns.

The village was not a large one, and the little crowd that was sighted astern next morning disappeared after the first shot from the cannon in the stern. At first Shard made the oxen wear rough iron bits, another of his mistakes, and strong bits too, "For if they run away," he had said, "we might as well be driving before a gale, and there's no saying where we'd find ourselves," but after a day or two he found that the bits were no good and, like the practical man he was, immediately corrected his mistake.

And now the crew sang merry songs all day, bringing out mandolins and clarionettes and cheering Captain Shard. All were jolly except the captain himself whose face was moody and perplexed; he alone expected to hear more of those villagers; and the oxen were drinking up the water every day; he alone feared that there was no more to be had, and a very unpleasant fear that is when your ship is becalmed in a desert. For over a week they went on like this, doing ten knots a day, and the music and singing got on the captain's nerves, but he dared not tell his men what the trouble was. And then one day the oxen drank up the last of the water. And Lieutenant Smerdrak came and reported the fact.

"Give them rum," said Shard, and he cursed the oxen. "What is good enough for me," he said, "should be good enough for them," and he swore that they should have rum.

"Aye, aye, sir," said the young lieutenant of pirates.

Shard should not be judged by the orders he gave that day; for nearly a fortnight he had watched the doom that was coming slowly towards him, discipline cut him off from anyone that might have shared his fear and discussed it, and all the while he had had to navigate his ship, which even at sea is an arduous responsibility. These things had fretted the calm of that clear judgment that had once baffled five navies. Therefore he cursed the oxen and ordered them rum, and Smerdrak had said "Aye, aye, sir," and gone below.

Towards sunset Shard was standing on the poop, thinking of death; it would not come to him by thirst; mutiny first, he thought. The oxen were refusing rum for the last time, and the men were beginning to eye Captain Shard in a very ominous way, not muttering, but each man looking at him with a side-long look of the eye as though there were only one thought among them all that had no need of words. A score of geese like a long letter "V" were crossing the evening sky, they slanted their necks and all went twisting downwards somewhere about the horizon. Captain Shard rushed to his chart-room, and presently the men came in at the door with Old Frank in front looking awkward and twisting his cap in his hand.

"What is it?" said Shard as though nothing were wrong.

Then Old Frank said what he had come to say: "We want to know what you be going to do."

And the men nodded grimly.

"Get water for the oxen," said Captain Shard, "as the swine won't have rum, and they'll have to work for it, the lazy beasts. Up anchor!"

And at the word water a look came into their faces like when some wanderer suddenly thinks of home.

"Water!" they said.

"Why not?" said Captain Shard. And none of them ever knew
that but for those geese, that slanted their necks and suddenly
twisted downwards, they would have found no water that
night nor ever after, and the Sahara would have taken them as
she has taken so many and shall take so many more. All that
night they followed their new course: at dawn they found an
oasis and the oxen drank.

And here, on this green acre or so with its palm trees and its
well, beleaguered by thousands of miles of desert and holding out
through the ages, here they decided to stay: for those who have
been without water for a while in one of Africa's deserts come to
have for that simple fluid such a regard as you, O reader, might
not easily credit. And here each man chose a site where he would
build his hut, and settle down, and marry perhaps, and even forget the sea; when Captain Shard having filled his tanks and barrels peremptorily ordered them to weigh anchor. There was
much dissatisfaction, even some grumbling, but when a man has
twice saved his fellows from death by the sheer freshness of his
mind they come to have a respect for his judgment that is not
shaken by trifles. It must be remembered that in the affair of the
dropping of the wind and again when they ran out of water these
men were at their wits' end: so was Shard on the last occasion,
but that they did not know. All this Shard knew, and he chose
this occasion to strengthen the reputation that he had in the
minds of the men of that bad ship by explaining to them his
motives, which usually he kept secret. The oasis, he said, must
be a port of call for all the travellers within hundreds of miles:
how many men did you see gathered together in any part of the
world where there was a drop of whiskey to be had! And water
here was rarer than whiskey in decent countries and, such was
the peculiarity of the Arabs, even more precious. Another thing
he pointed out to them, the Arabs were a singularly inquisitive
people and if they came upon a ship in the desert they would
probably talk about it; and the world having a wickedly mali-
cious tongue would never construe in its proper light their difference with the English and Spanish fleets, but would merely
side with the strong against the weak.

And the men sighed, and sang the capstan song, and hoisted
the anchor and yoked the oxen up, and away they went doing
their steady knot, which nothing could increase. It may be
thought strange that with all sail furled in dead calm and
while the oxen rested they should have cast anchor at all. But

custom is not easily overcome and long survives its use. Rather enquire how many such useless customs we ourselves preserve: the flaps, for instance, to pull up the tops of hunting boots though the tops no longer pull up, the bows on our evening shoes that neither tie nor untie. They said they felt safer that way, and there was an end of it.

Shard lay a course of south by west and they did ten knots that day, the next day they did seven or eight and Shard hove to. Here he intended to stop; they had huge supplies of fodder on board for the oxen, for his men he had a pig or so, plenty of poultry, several sacks of biscuits and ninety-eight oxen (for two were already eaten), and they were only twenty miles from water. Here he said they would stay till folks forgot their past, someone would invent something or some new thing would turn up to take folks' minds off them and the ships he had sunk: he forgot that there are men who are well paid to remember.

Half-way between him and the oasis he established a little depot where he buried his water-barrels. As soon as a barrel was empty he sent half a dozen men to roll it by turns to the depot. This they would do at night, keeping hid by day, and next night they would push on to the oasis, fill the barrel and roll it back. Thus only ten miles away he soon had a store of water, unknown to the thirstiest native of Africa, from which he could safely replenish his tanks at will. He allowed his men to sing and even within reason to light fires. Those were jolly nights while the rum held out; sometimes they saw gazelles watching them curiously, sometimes a lion went by over the sand, the sound of his roar added to their sense of the security of their ship; all round them level, immense lay the Sahara. "This is better than an English prison," said Captain Shard.

And still the dead calm lasted, not even the sand whispered at night to little winds; and when the rum gave out and it looked like trouble, Shard reminded them what little use it had been to them when it was all they had and the oxen wouldn't look at it.

And the days wore on with singing, and even dancing at times, and at nights round a cautious fire in a hollow of sand, with only one man on watch, they told tales of the sea. It was all a relief after arduous watches and sleeping by the guns, a rest to strained nerves and eyes; and all agreed, for all that they missed their rum, that the best place for a ship like theirs was the land.

This was in latitude 23 north, longitude 4 east, where, as I have said, a ship's broadside was heard for the first time and the last. It happened this way.

They had been there several weeks and had eaten perhaps ten or a dozen oxen and all that while there had been no breath of wind and they had seen no one: when one morning about two bells when the crew were at breakfast the look-out man reported cavalry on the port side. Shard, who had already surrounded his ship with sharpened stakes, ordered all his men on board; the young trumpeter, who prided himself on having picked up the ways of the land, sounded "Prepare to receive cavalry"; Shard sent a few men below with pikes to the lower port-holes, two more aloft with muskets, the rest to the guns; he changed the "grape" or "canister" with which the guns were loaded in case of a surprise, for shot, cleared the decks, drew in ladders, and before the cavalry came within range everything was ready for them. The oxen were always yoked in order that Shard could manœuvre his ship at a moment's notice.

When first sighted the cavalry were trotting, but they were coming on now at a slow canter. Arabs in white robes on good horses. Shard estimated that there were two or three hundred of them. At six hundred yards Shard opened with one gun; he had had the distance measured, but had never practised for fear of being heard at the oasis: the shot went high. The next one fell short and ricochetted over the Arabs' heads. Shard had the range then, and by the time the ten remaining guns of his broadside were given the same elevation as that of his second gun the Arabs had come to the spot where the last shot pitched. The broadside hit the horses, mostly low, and ricochetted on amongst them; one cannon-ball striking a rock at the horses' feet shattered it and sent fragments flying amongst the Arabs with the peculiar scream of things set free by projectiles from their motionless harmless state, and the cannon-ball went on with them with a great howl; this shot alone killed three men.

"Very satisfactory," said Shard, rubbing his chin. "Load with grape," he added sharply.

The broadside did not stop the Arabs nor even reduce their speed, but they crowded in closer together as though for company in their time of danger, which they should not have done. They were four hundred yards off now, three hundred and

fifty; and then the muskets began, for the two men in the
crow's-nest had thirty loaded muskets besides a few pistols;
the muskets all stood round them leaning against the rail;
they picked them up and fired them one by one. Every shot
told, but still the Arabs came on. They were galloping now. It
took some time to load the guns in those days. Three hundred
yards, two hundred and fifty, men dropping all the way, two
hundred yards; Old Frank for all his one ear had terrible eyes;
it was pistols now, they had fired all their muskets; a hundred
and fifty; Shard had marked the fifties with little white stones.
Old Frank and Bad Jack up aloft felt pretty uneasy when they
saw the Arabs had come to that little white stone, they both
missed their shots.

"All ready?" said Captain Shard.

"Aye, aye, sir," said Smerdrak.

"Right," said Captain Shard, raising a finger.

A hundred and fifty yards is a bad range at which to be
caught by grape (or "case" as we call it now), the gunners can
hardly miss and the charge has time to spread. Shard estimated afterwards that he got thirty Arabs by that broadside
alone and as many horses.

There were close on two hundred of them still on their
horses, yet the broadside of grape had unsettled them, they
surged round the ship but seemed doubtful what to do. They
carried swords and scimitars in their hands, though most had
strange long muskets slung behind them; a few unslung them
and began firing wildly. They could not reach Shard's merry
men with their swords. Had it not been for that broadside that
took them when it did they might have climbed up from their
horses and carried the bad ship by sheer force of numbers, but
they would have had to have been very steady, and the broadside spoiled all that. Their best course was to have concentrated all their efforts in setting fire to the ship, but this they
did not attempt. Part of them swarmed all round the ship
brandishing their swords and looking vainly for an easy
entrance; perhaps they expected a door, they were not seafar-
ing people; but their leaders were evidently set on driving off
the oxen, not dreaming that the *Desperate Lark* had other
means of travelling. And this to some extent they succeeded in
doing. Thirty they drove off, cutting the traces, twenty they
killed on the spot with their scimitars though the bow gun
caught them twice as they did their work, and ten more were

unluckily killed by Shard's bow gun. Before they could fire a third time from the bows they all galloped away, firing back at the oxen with their muskets and killing three more, and what troubled Shard more than the loss of his oxen was the way that they manœuvred, galloping off just when the bow gun was ready and riding off by the port bow where the broadside could not get them, which seemed to him to show more knowledge of guns than they could have learned on that bright morning. What, thought Shard to himself, if they should bring big guns against the *Desperate Lark*! And the mere thought of it made him rail at Fate. But the merry men all cheered when they rode away. Shard had only twenty-two oxen left, and then a score or so of the Arabs dismounted while the rest rode further on leading their horses. And the dismounted men lay down on the port bow behind some rocks two hundred yards away and began to shoot at the oxen. Shard had just enough of them left to manœuvre his ship with an effort, and he turned his ship a few points to the starboard so as to get a broadside at the rocks. But grape was of no use here, as the only way he could get an Arab was by hitting one of the rocks with shot behind which an Arab was lying, and the rocks were not easy to hit except by chance, and as often as he manœuvred his ship the Arabs changed their ground. This went on all day while the mounted Arabs hovered out of range watching what Shard would do; and all the while the oxen were growing fewer, so good a mark were they, until only ten were left and the ship could manœuvre no longer. But then they all rode off.

The merry men were delighted, they calculated that one way and another they had unhorsed a hundred Arabs, and on board there had been no more than one man wounded: Bad Jack had been hit in the wrist; probably by a bullet meant for the men at the guns, for the Arabs were firing high. They had captured a horse and had found quaint weapons on the bodies of the dead Arabs and an interesting kind of tobacco. It was evening now and they talked over the fight, made jokes about their luckier shots, smoked their new tobacco and sang: altogether it was the jolliest evening they'd had. But Shard alone on the quarter-deck paced to and fro pondering, brooding and wondering. He had chopped off Bad Jack's wounded hand and given him a hook out of store, for captain does doctor upon these occasions, and Shard, who was ready for most things, kept half a dozen or so of neat new limbs, and of course a chop-

per. Bad Jack had gone below swearing a little and said he'd
lie down for a bit, the men were smoking and singing on the
sand, and Shard was there alone. The thought that troubled
Shard was: What would the Arabs do? They did not look like
men to go away for nothing. And at back of all his thoughts
was one that reiterated guns, guns, guns. He argued with himself that they could not drag them all that way on the sand,
that the *Desperate Lark* was not worth it, that they had given
it up. Yet he knew in his heart that that was what they would
do. He knew there were fortified towns in Africa, and as for its
being worth it, he knew that there was no pleasant thing left
now to those defeated men except revenge, and if the *Desperate
Lark* had come over the sand, why not guns? He knew that the
ship could never hold out against guns and cavalry, a week
perhaps, two weeks, even three: what difference did it make
how long it was? And the men sang:

> Away we go,
> Oho, Oho, Oho,
> A drop of rum for you and me,
> And the world's as round as the letter O,
> And round it runs the sea.

A melancholy settled down on Shard.

About sunset Lieutenant Smerdrak came up for orders.
Shard ordered a trench to be dug along the port side of the
ship. The men wanted to sing and grumbled at having to dig,
especially as Shard never mentioned his fear of guns, but he
fingered his pistols and in the end Shard had his way. No one
on board could shoot like Captain Shard. That is often the way
with captains of pirate ships, it is a difficult position to hold.
Discipline is essential to those that have the right to fly the
skull-and-cross-bones, and Shard was the man to enforce it. It
was starlight by the time the trench was dug to the captain's
satisfaction, and the men that it was to protect when the worst
came to the worst swore all the time as they dug. And when it
was finished they clamoured to make a feast on some of the
killed oxen, and this Shard let them do. And they lit a huge fire
for the first time, burning abundant scrub, they thinking that
the Arabs daren't return, Shard knowing that concealment
was now useless. All that night they feasted and sang, and
Shard sat up in his chart-room making his plans.

When morning came they rigged up the cutter, as they called
the captured horse, and told off her crew. As there were only

two men that could ride at all these became the crew of the cutter. Spanish Dick and Bill the Boatswain were the two.

Shard's orders were that turn and turn about they should
take command of the cutter and cruise about five miles off to
the north-east all the day, but at night they were to come in.
And they fitted the horse up with a flagstaff in front of the saddle so that they could signal from her, and carried an anchor
behind for fear she should run away.

And as soon as Spanish Dick had ridden off Shard sent some
men to roll all the barrels back from the depot, where they
were buried in the sand, with orders to watch the cutter all the
time, and, if she signalled, to return as fast as they could.

They buried the Arabs that day, removing their water-bottles
and any provisions they had, and that night they got all the
water-barrels in, and for days nothing happened. One event of
extraordinary importance did indeed occur: the wind got up
one day, but it was due south, and as the oasis lay to the north
of them, and beyond that they might pick up the camel track,
Shard decided to stay where he was. If it had looked to him
like lasting Shard might have hoisted sail, but it dropped at
evening as he knew it would, and in any case it was not the
wind he wanted. And more days went by, two weeks without a
breeze. The dead oxen would not keep and they had had to kill
three more; there were only seven left now.

Never before had the men been so long without rum. And
Captain Shard had doubled the watch, besides making two
more men sleep at the guns. They had tired of their simple
games, and most of their songs; and their tales that were never
true were no longer new. And then one day the monotony of the
desert came down upon them.

There is a fascination in the Sahara: a day there is delightful, a week is pleasant, a fortnight is a matter of opinion, but
it was running into months. The men were perfectly polite, but
the boatswain wanted to know when Shard thought of moving
on. It was an unreasonable question to ask of the captain of
any ship in a dead calm in a desert, but Shard said he would
set a course and let him know in a day or two. And a day or two
went by over the monotony of the Sahara, who for monotony is
unequalled by all the parts of the earth. Great marshes cannot
equal it, nor plains of grass nor the sea; the Sahara alone lies
unaltered by the seasons, she has no altering surface, no flowers to fade or grow, year in year out she is changeless for hun-

dreds and hundreds of miles. And the boatswain came again and took off his cap and asked Captain Shard to be so kind as to tell them about his new course. Shard said he meant to stay until they had eaten three more of the oxen as they could only take three of them in the hold, there were only six left now. But what if there was no wind? the boatswain said. And at that moment the faintest breeze from the north ruffled the boatswain's forelock as he stood with his cap in his hand.

"Don't talk about the wind to *me*," said Captain Shard: and Bill was a little frightened for Shard's mother had been a gipsy.

But it was only a breeze astray, a trick of the Sahara. And another week went by and they ate two more oxen.

They obeyed Captain Shard ostentatiously now, but they wore ominous looks. Bill came again and Shard answered him in Romany.

Things were like this one hot Sahara morning when the cutter signalled. The look-out man told Shard and Shard read the message. "Cavalry astern" it read, and then a little later she signalled "With guns."

"Ah," said Captain Shard.

One ray of hope Shard had; the flags on the cutter fluttered. For the first time for five weeks a light breeze blew from the north, very light, you hardly felt it. Spanish Dick rode in and anchored his horse to starboard and the cavalry came on slowly from the port.

Not till the afternoon did they come in sight, and all the while that little breeze was blowing.

"One knot," said Shard at noon. "Two knots," he said at six bells, and still it grew and the Arabs trotted nearer. By five o'clock the merry men of the bad ship *Desperate Lark* could make out twelve long old-fashioned guns on low-wheeled carts dragged by horses, and what looked like lighter guns carried on camels. The wind was blowing a little stronger now.

"Shall we hoist sail, sir?" said Bill.

"Not yet," said Shard.

By six o'clock the Arabs were just outside the range of cannon and there they halted. Then followed an anxious hour or so, but the Arabs came no nearer. They evidently meant to wait till dark to bring their guns up. Probably they intended to dig a gun epaulement from which they could safely pound away at the ship.

"We could do three knots," said Shard half to himself, he was walking up and down his quarter-deck with very fast short paces. And then the sun set and they heard the Arabs praying, and Shard's merry men cursed at the top of their voices to show that they were as good men as they.

The Arabs had come no nearer, waiting for night. They did not know how Shard was longing for it too, he was gritting his teeth and sighing for it, he even would have prayed, but that he feared that it might remind Heaven of him and his merry men.

Night came and the stars. "Hoist sail," said Shard. The men sprang to their places, they had had enough of that silent lonely spot. They took the oxen on board and let the great sails down; and like a lover coming from over sea, long dreamed of, long expected, like a lost friend seen again after many years, the north wind came into the pirates' sails. And before Shard could stop it a ringing English cheer went away to the wondering Arabs.

They started off at three knots, and soon they might have done four, but Shard would not risk it at night. All night the wind held good, and doing three knots from ten to four they were far out of sight of the Arabs when daylight came. And then Shard hoisted more sail and they did four knots, and by eight bells they were doing four and a half. The spirits of those volatile men rose high, and discipline became perfect. So long as there was wind in the sails and water in the tanks Captain Shard felt safe at least from mutiny. Great men can only be overthrown while their fortunes are at their lowest. Having failed to depose Shard when his plans were open to criticism and he himself scarce knew what to do next, it was hardly likely they could do it now; and whatever we think of his past and his way of living we cannot deny that Shard was among the great men of the world.

Of defeat by the Arabs he did not feel so sure. It was useless to try to cover his tracks even if he had had time, the Arab cavalry could have picked them up anywhere. And he was afraid of their camels with those light guns on board, he had heard they could do seven knots and keep it up most of the day, and if as much as one shot struck the mainmast . . . and Shard taking his mind off useless fears worked out on his chart when the Arabs were likely to overtake them. He told his men that the wind would hold good for a week, and, gipsy or no, he certainly knew as much about the wind as is good for a sailor to know.

Alone in his chart-room he worked it out like this: mark two hours to the good for surprise and finding the tracks and delay in starting, say three hours if the guns were mounted in their epaulements, then the Arabs should start at seven. Supposing the camels go twelve hours a day at seven knots they would do eighty-four knots a day, while Shard doing three knots from ten to four, and four knots the rest of the time, was doing ninety and actually gaining. But when it came to it he would-n't risk more than two knots at night while the enemy were out of sight, for he rightly regarded anything more than that as dangerous when sailing on land at night, so he too did eighty-four knots a day. It was a pretty race. I have not troubled to see if Shard added up his figures wrongly or if he underrated the pace of camels, but whatever it was the Arabs gained slightly, for on the fourth day Spanish Jack, five knots astern on what they called the cutter, sighted the camels a very long way off and signalled the fact to Shard. They had left their cavalry behind as Shard supposed they would. The wind held good, they had still two oxen left, and could always eat their "cutter," and they had a fair, though not ample, supply of water; but the appearance of the Arabs was a blow to Shard, for it showed him that there was no getting away from them, and of all things he dreaded guns. He made light of it to the men: said they would sink the lot before they had been in action half an hour: yet he feared that once the guns came up it was only a question of time before his rigging was cut or his steering gear disabled.

One point the *Desperate Lark* scored over the Arabs and a very good one too, darkness fell just before they could have sighted her, and now Shard used the lantern ahead as he dared not do on the first night when the Arabs were close, and with the help of it managed to do three knots. The Arabs encamped in the evening and the *Desperate Lark* gained twenty knots. But the next evening they appeared again, and this time they saw the sails of the *Desperate Lark*.

On the sixth day they were close. On the seventh they were closer. And then, a line of verdure across their bows, Shard saw the Niger River.

Whether he knew that for a thousand miles it rolled its course through forest, whether he even knew that it was there at all; what his plans were, or whether he lived from day to day like a man whose days are numbered, he never told his men.

Nor can I get an indication on this point from the talk that I hear from sailors in their cups in a certain tavern I know of. His face was expressionless, his mouth shut, and he held his ship to her course. That evening they were up to the edge of the tree-trunks and the Arabs camped and waited ten knots astern, and the wind had sunk a little.

There Shard anchored a little before sunset and landed at once. At first he explored the forest a little on foot. Then he sent for Spanish Dick. They had slung the cutter on board some days ago when they found she could not keep up. Shard could not ride, but he sent for Spanish Disk and told him he must take him as a passenger. So Spanish Dick slung him in front of the saddle "before the mast," as Shard called it, for they still carried a mast on the front of the saddle, and away they galloped together. "Rough weather," said Shard, but he surveyed the forest as he went, and the long and short of it was he found a place where the forest was less than half a mile thick and the *Desperate Lark* might get through: but twenty trees must be cut. Shard marked the trees himself, sent Spanish Dick right back to watch the Arabs and turned the whole of his crew on to those twenty trees. It was a frightful risk, the *Desperate Lark* was empty, with an enemy no more than ten knots astern, but it was a moment for bold measures and Shard took the chance of being left without his ship in the heart of Africa in the hope of being repaid by escaping altogether.

The men worked all night long on those twenty trees, those that had no axes bored with bradawls and blasted, and then relieved those that had.

Shard was indefatigable, he went from tree to tree, showing exactly what way every one was to fall, and what was to be done with them when they were down. Some had to be cut down because their branches would get in the way of the masts, others because their trunks would be in the way of the wheels; in the case of the last the stumps had to be made smooth and low with saws and perhaps a bit of the trunk sawn off and rolled away. This was the hardest work they had. And they were all large trees; on the other hand, had they been small, there would have been many more of them and they could not have sailed in and out, sometimes for hundreds of yards, without cutting any at all: and all this Shard calculated on doing if only there was time.

The light before dawn came and it looked as if they would never do it at all. And then dawn came and it was all done but one tree, the hard part of the work had all been done in the night and a sort of final rush cleared everything up except that one huge tree. And then the cutter signalled the Arabs were moving. At dawn they had prayed, and now they had struck their camp. Shard at once ordered all his men to the ship except ten whom he left at the tree; they had some way to go and the Arabs had been moving some ten minutes before they got there. Shard took in the cutter, which wasted five minutes, hoisted sail short-handed and that took five minutes more, and slowly got under way.

The wind was dropping still, and by the time the *Desperate Lark* had come to the edge of that part of the forest through which Shard had laid his course the Arabs were no more than five knots away. He had sailed east half a mile, which he ought to have done overnight so as to be ready, but he could not spare time or thought or men away from those twenty trees. Then Shard turned into the forest and the Arabs were dead astern. They hurried when they saw the *Desperate Lark* enter the forest.

"Doing ten knots," said Shard as he watched them from the deck. The *Desperate Lark* was doing no more than a knot and a half, for the wind was weak under the lee of the trees. Yet all went well for a while. The big tree had just come down some way ahead, and the ten men were sawing bits off the trunk.

And then Shard saw a branch that he had not marked on the chart, it would just catch the top of the mainmast. He anchored at once and sent a hand aloft who sawed it half-way through and did the rest with a pistol, and now the Arabs were only three knots astern. For a quarter of a mile Shard steered them through the forest till they came to the ten men and that bad big tree; another foot had yet to come off one corner of the stump, for the wheels had to pass over it. Shard turned all hands on to the stump, and it was then that the Arabs came within shot. But they had to unpack their gun. And before they had it mounted Shard was away. If they had charged things might have been different. When they saw the *Desperate Lark* under way again the Arabs came on to within three hundred yards and there they mounted two guns. Shard watched them along his stern gun but would not fire. They were six hundred yards away before the Arabs could fire, and then they fired too

soon and both guns missed. And Shard and his merry men saw
clear water only ten fathoms ahead. Then Shard loaded his
stern gun with canister instead of shot and at the same
moment the Arabs charged on their camels; they came galloping down through the forest waving long lances. Shard left the
steering to Smerdrak and stood by the stern gun; the Arabs
were within fifty yards and still Shard did not fire; he had
most of his men in the stern with muskets beside him. Those
lances carried on camels were altogether different from swords
in the hands of horsemen, they could reach the men on deck.
The men could see the horrible barbs on the lance-heads, they
were almost at their faces when Shard fired; and at the same
moment the *Desperate Lark* with her dry and sun-cracked keel
in air on the high bank of the Niger fell forward like a diver.
The gun went off through the tree-tops, a wave came over the
bows and swept the stern, the *Desperate Lark* wriggled and
righted herself, she was back in her element.

The merry men looked at the wet decks and at their dripping
clothes. "Water," they said almost wonderingly.

The Arabs followed a little way through the forest, but when
they saw that they had to face a broadside instead of one stern
gun and perceived that a ship afloat is less vulnerable to cavalry even than when on shore, they abandoned ideas of
revenge, and comforted themselves with a text out of their
sacred book which tells how in other days and other places our
enemies shall suffer even as we desire.

For a thousand miles with the flow of the Niger and the help
of occasional winds, the *Desperate Lark* moved seawards. At
first he sweeps east a little and then southwards, till you come
to Akassa and the open sea.

I will not tell you how they caught fish and ducks, raided a
village here and there and at last came to Akassa, for I have
said much already of Captain Shard. Imagine them drawing
nearer and nearer the sea, bad men all, and yet with a feeling
for something where we feel for our king, our country or our
home, a feeling for something that burned in them not less
ardently than our feelings in us, and that something the sea.
Imagine them nearing it till sea birds appeared and they fancied they felt sea breezes and all sang songs again that they
had not sung for weeks. Imagine them heaving at last on the
salt Atlantic again.

I have said much already of Captain Shard and I fear lest I

shall weary you, O my reader, if I tell you any more of so bad a man. I, too, at the top of a tower all alone am weary.

And yet it is right that such a tale should be told. A journey almost due south from near Algiers to Akassa in a ship that we should call no more than a yacht. Let it be a stimulus to younger men.

GUARANTEE TO THE READER

Since writing down for your benefit, O my reader, all this long tale that I heard in the tavern by the sea, I have travelled in Algeria and Tunisia as well as in the Desert. Much that I saw in those countries seems to throw doubt on the tale that the sailor told me. To begin with, the Desert does not come within hundreds of miles of the coast, and there are more mountains to cross than you would suppose, the Atlas mountains in particular. It is just possible Shard might have got through by El Cantara, following the camel road which is many centuries old; or he may have gone by Algiers and Bou Saada and through the mountain pass El Finita Dem, though that is a bad enough way for camels to go (let alone bullocks with a ship), for which reason the Arabs call it Finita Dem—the Path of Blood.

I should not have ventured to give this story the publicity of print had the sailor been sober when he told it, for fear that he should have deceived you, O my reader; but this was never the case with him, as I took good care to ensure: *in vino veritas* is a sound old proverb, and I never had cause to doubt his word unless that proverb lies.

If it should prove that he has deceived me, let it pass; but if he has been the means of deceiving you, there are little things about him that I know, the common gossip of that ancient tavern whose leaded bottle-glass windows watch the sea, which I will tell at once to every judge of my acquaintance, and it will be a pretty race to see which of them will hang him.

Meanwhile, O my reader, believe the story, resting assured that if you are taken in the thing shall be a matter for the hangman.

The Loot of Loma

A TALE OF AN INDIAN ADVENTURE

Coming back laden with the loot of Loma, the four tall men looked earnestly to the right; to the left they durst not, for the precipice there that had been with them so long went sickly down on to a bank of clouds, and how much further below that only their fears could say.

Loma lay smoking a city of ruin behind them, all its defenders dead, there was no one left to pursue them; and yet their Indian instincts told them that all was scarcely well. They had gone three days along that narrow ledge, mountain quite smooth, incredible above them, and precipice as smooth and as far below. It was chilly there in the mountains; at night a stream or a wind in the gloom of the chasm below them went like a whisper; the stillness of all things else began to wear the nerve, an enemy's howl would have braced them; they began to wish their perilous path were wider, they began to wish that they had not sacked Loma.

Had that path been any wider the sacking of Loma must indeed have been harder for them, for the citizens must have fortified the city but that the awful narrowness of that ten-league pass of the hills had made their crag-surrounded city secure. And at last an Indian had said, "Come, let us sack it." Grimly they laughed in the wigwams. Only the eagles, they said, had ever seen it, its hoard of emeralds and its golden gods. And one had said he would reach it; and they answered, "Only the eagles."

It was Laughing Face who said it and who gathered thirty braves and led them into Loma with their tomahawks and their bows; there were only four left now, but they had the loot of Loma on a mule. They had four golden gods, a hundred emeralds, fifty-two rubies, a large silver gong, two sticks of malachite with amethyst handles for holding incense at religious feasts, four beakers one foot high, each carved from a rose-quartz crystal, a little coffer carved out of two diamonds, and (had they but known it) the written curse of a priest. It was written on parchment in an unknown tongue and had been slipped in with the loot by a dying hand.

From either end of that narrow terrible ledge the third night was closing in; it was dropping down on them from the heights of the mountain and slipping up to them out of the abyss, the third night since Loma blazed and they had left it. Three more days of tramping should bring them in triumph home, and yet their instincts said that all was scarcely well. We who sit at home and draw the blinds and shut the shutters as soon as night appears, who gather round the fire when the wind is wild, who pray at regular seasons and in familiar shrines, know little of the demoniac look of night when it is filled with curses of false infuriate gods. Such a night was this. Though in the heights the fleecy clouds were idle yet the wind was stirring mournfully in the abyss and moaning as it stirred, unhappily at first and full of sorrow, but as day turned away from that awful path a very definite menace entered its voice which fast grew louder and louder, and night came on with a long howl. Shadows repeatedly passed over the stars, and then a mist fell swiftly, as though there were something suddenly to be done and utterly to be hidden, as in very truth there was.

And in the chill of that mist the four tall men prayed to their totems, the whimsical wooden figures that stood so far away, watching the pleasant wigwams; the firelight even now would be dancing over their faces, while there would come to their ears delectable tales of war. They halted upon the pass and prayed, and waited for any sign. For a man's totem may be in the likeness perhaps of an otter, and a man may pray, and if his totem be placable and watching over his man a noise may be heard at once like the noise that the otter makes, though it be but a stone that falls on another stone; and the noise is a sign. The four men's totems that stood so far away were in the likeness of the coney, the bear, the heron and the lizard. They waited and no sign came. With all the noises of the wind in the abyss no noise was like the thump that the coney makes, nor the bear's growl nor the heron's screech nor the rustle of the lizard in the reeds.

It seemed that the wind was saying something over and over again and that that thing was evil. They prayed again to their totems; and no sign came. And then they knew that there was some power that night that was prevailing against the pleas-

ant carvings on painted poles of wood with the firelight on
their faces so far away. Now it was clear that the wind was saying something, some very, very dreadful thing in a tongue that
they did not know. They listened, but you could not tell what it
said. Nobody could have said from seeing their faces how much
the four tall men desired the wigwams again, desired the
campfire and the tales of war, and the benignant totems that
listened and smiled in the dusk. Nobody could have seen how
well they knew that this was no common night or wholesome
mist.

When at last no answer came nor any sign from their totems
they pulled out of the bag those golden gods that Loma gave
not up except in flames and when all her men were dead. They
had large ruby eyes and emerald tongues. They set them down
upon that mountain pass, the cross-legged idols with their
emerald tongues, and having placed between them a few
decent yards, as it seemed meet there should be between gods
and men, they bowed them down and prayed in their desperate straits in that dank ominous night to the gods they had
wronged; for it seemed that there was a vengeance upon the
hills and that they would scarce escape, as the wind knew well.
And the gods laughed, all four, and wagged their emerald
tongues; the Indians saw them though the night had fallen
and though the mist was low. The four tall men leaped up at
once from their knees, and would have left the gods upon the
pass, but that they feared some hunter of their tribe might one
day find them and say of Laughing Face, "He fled and left
behind his golden gods," and sell the gold, and come with his
wealth to the wigwams, and be greater than Laughing Face
and his three men. And then they would have cast the gods
away, down the abyss with their eyes and their emerald
tongues; but they knew that enough already they had wronged
Loma's gods, and feared that vengeance enough was waiting
them on the hills. So they packed them back in the bag on the
frightened mule, the bag that held the curse they knew nothing of, and so pushed on into the menacing night. Till midnight
they plodded on and would not sleep; grimmer and grimmer
grew the look of the night and the wind more full of meaning,
and the mule knew and trembled, and it seemed that the wind
knew too, as did the instincts of those four tall men, though
they could not reason it out try how they would.

And though the squaws waited long where the pass winds

out of the mountains, near where the wigwams are upon the plains, the wigwams and the totems and the fire, and though they watched by day, and for many nights uttered familiar calls, still did they never see those four tall men emerge out the mountains any more, even though they prayed to their totems upon their painted poles; but the curse in the mystical writing that they had unknown in their bag worked there on that lonely pass six leagues from the ruins of Loma, and nobody can tell us what it was.

A Tale of the Equator

He who is sultan so remote to the East that his dominions were deemed fabulous in Babylon, whose name is a byword for distance to-day in the streets of Bagdad, whose capital bearded travellers invoke by name in the gate at evening to gather hearers to their tales, when the smoke of tobacco arises, dice rattle and taverns shine; even he in that very city made mandate and said: "Let there be brought hither all my learned men that they may come before me and rejoice my heart with learning."

Men ran and clarions sounded and it was so that there came before the sultan all of his learned men. And many were found wanting. But of those that were able to say acceptable things, ever after to be named The Fortunate, one said that to the South of the Earth lay a Land—said and was crowned with lotus—where it was summer in our winter days and where it was winter in summer.

And when the sultan of those most distant lands knew that the Creator of All had contrived a device so vastly to his delight, his merriment knew no bounds. On a sudden he spake and said, and this was the gist of his saying, that upon that line of boundary or limit that divided the North from the South a palace be made, where in the Northern courts should summer be, while in the South was winter; so should he move from court to court according to his mood, and dally with the summer in the morning and spend the noon with snow. So the sultan's poets were sent for and bade to tell of that city, foreseeing its splendour far away to the South and in the future of time; and some were found fortunate. And of those that were found fortunate and were crowned with flowers none earned more easily the sultan's smile (on which long days depended) than he that foreseeing the city spake of it thus:

"In seven years and seven days, O Prop of Heaven, shall thy builders build it, thy palace that is neither North nor South, where neither summer nor winter is sole lord of the hours.

White I see it, very vast as a city, very fair as a woman, Earth's wonder, with many windows, with thy princesses peering out at twilight; yea I behold the bliss of the gold balconies, and hear a rustling down long galleries and the doves' coo upon its sculptured eaves. O Prop of Heaven, would that so fair a city were built by thine ancient sires, the children of the sun, that so might all men see it even to-day and not the poets only, whose vision sees it so far away to the South and in the future of time.

"O King of the years, it shall stand midmost on that line that divideth equally the North from the South and that parteth the seasons asunder as with a screen. On the northern side when summer is in the North thy silken guards shall pace by dazzling walls while thy spearmen clad in furs go round the South. But at the hour of noon in the midmost day of the year thy chamberlain shall go down from his high place and into the midmost court, and men with trumpets shall go down behind him, and he shall utter a great cry at noon, and the men with trumpets shall cause their trumpets to blare, and the spearmen clad in furs shall march to the North and thy silken guard shall take their place in the South, and summer shall leave the North and go to the South, and all the swallows shall rise and follow after. And alone in thine inner courts shall no change be, for they shall lie narrowly along that line that parteth the seasons in sunder and divideth the North from the South, and thy long gardens shall lie under them.

"And in thy gardens shall spring always be, for spring lies ever at the marge of summer, and autumn also shall always tint thy gardens, for autumn always flares at winter's edge, and those gardens shall lie apart between winter and summer. And there shall be orchards in thy garden too, with all the burden of autumn on their boughs and all the blossom of spring.

"Yea I behold this palace, for we see future things; I see its white wall shine in the huge glare of mid summer, and the lizards lying along it motionless in the sun, and men asleep in the noonday, and the butterflies floating by, and birds of radiant plumage chasing marvellous moths; far off the forest, and great orchids glorying there, and iridescent insects dancing round in the light. I see the wall upon the other side, the snow has come upon the battlements, the icicles have fringed them like frozen beards, a wild wind blowing out of lonely places and crying to the cold fields as it blows has sent the snowdrifts higher than the buttresses; they that look out through windows on that side of thy palace see the wild geese flying low and all the birds of the winter, going by swift in packs beat low by the bitter wind, and the clouds above them are black for it is midwinter there: while in thine other courts the fountains tinkle, falling on marble warmed by the fire of the summer sun.

"Such, O King of the years, shall thy palace be, and its name shall be Erlathdronion, Earth's Wonder, and thy wisdom shall bid thine architects build at once that all may see what as yet the poets see only, and that prophecy be fulfilled."

And when the poet ceased the sultan spake, and said as all men hearkened with bent heads:

"It will be unnecessary for my builders to build this palace, Erlathdronion, Earth's Wonder, for in hearing thee we have drunk already its pleasures."

And the poet went forth from the Presence and dreamed a new thing.

A Narrow Escape

It was underground.

In that dank cavern down below Belgrave Square the walls were dripping. But what was that to the magician? It was secrecy that he needed, not dryness. There he pondered upon the trend of events, shaped destinies and concocted magical brews.

For the last few years the serenity of his ponderings had been disturbed by the noise of the motor-bus; while to his keen ears there came the earthquake-rumble, far off, of the train in the tube, going down Sloane Street; and what he heard of the world above his head was not to its credit.

He decided one evening over his evil pipe, down there in his dank dark chamber, that London had lived long enough, had abused its opportunities, had gone too far, in fine, with its civilization. And so he decided to wreck it.

Therefore he beckoned up his acolyte from the weedy end of the cavern, and, "Bring me," he said, "the heart of the toad that dwelleth in Arabia and by the mountains of Bethany." The acolyte slipped away by the hidden door, leaving that grim old man with his frightful pipe, and whither he went who knows but the gipsy people, or by what path he returned; but within a year he stood in the cavern again, slipping secretly in by the trap while the old man smoked, and he brought with him a little fleshy thing that rotted in a casket of pure gold.

"What is it?" the old man croaked.

"It is," said the acolyte, "the heart of the toad that dwelt once in Arabia and by the mountains of Bethany."

The old man's crooked fingers closed on it, and he blessed the acolyte with his rasping voice and claw-like hand uplifted; the motor-bus rumbled above on its endless journey; far off the train shook Sloane Street.

"Come," said the old magician, "it is time." And there and then they left the weedy cavern, the acolyte carrying cauldron, gold poker and all things needful, and went abroad in the light. And very wonderful the old man looked in his silks.

Their goal was the outskirts of London; the old man strode in front and the acolyte ran behind him, and there was something magical in the old man's stride alone, without his wonderful dress, the cauldron and wand, the hurrying acolyte and the small gold poker.

Little boys jeered till they caught the old man's eye. So there went on through London this strange procession of two, too swift for any to follow. Things seemed worse up there than they did in the cavern, and the further they got on their way towards London's outskirts the worse London got. "It is time," said the old man, "surely."

And so they came at last to London's edge and a small hill watching it with a mournful look. It was so mean that the acolyte longed for the cavern, dank though it was and full of terrible sayings that the old man said when he slept.

They climbed the hill and put the cauldron down, and put therein the necessary things, and lit a fire of herbs that no chemist will sell nor decent gardener grow, and stirred the cauldron with the golden poker. The magician retired a little apart and muttered, then he strode back to the cauldron and, all being ready, suddenly opened the casket and let the fleshy thing fall in to boil.

Then he made spells, *then* he flung up his arms; the fumes from the cauldron entering in at his mind he said raging things that he had not known before and runes that were dreadful (the acolyte screamed); there he cursed London from fog to loam-pit, from zenith to the abyss; motor-bus, factory, shop, parliament, people. "Let them all perish," he said, "and London pass away, tram lines and bricks and pavement, the usurpers too long of the fields, let them all pass away and the wild hares come back, blackberry and briar-rose.

"Let it pass," he said, "pass now, pass utterly."

In the momentary silence the old man coughed, then waited with eager eyes; and the long long hum of London hummed as it always has since first the reed-huts were set up by the river, changing its note at times but always humming, louder now than it was in years gone by, but humming night and day though its voice be cracked with age; so it hummed on.

And the old man turned him round to his trembling acolyte and terribly said as he sank into the earth: "YOU HAVE NOT BROUGHT ME THE HEART OF THE TOAD THAT DWELLETH IN ARABIA AND BY THE MOUNTAINS OF BETHANY!"

The Watch-Tower

I sat one April evening in Provence on a small hill above an ancient town that Goth and Vandal as yet have forborne to "bring up to date."

On the hill was an old worn castle with a watch-tower, and a well with narrow steps and water in it still.

The watch-tower staring south with neglected windows faced a broad valley full of the pleasant twilight and the hum of evening things: it saw the fires of wanderers blink from the hills, beyond them the long forest black with pines, one star appearing, and darkness settling slowly down on Var.

Sitting there listening to the green frogs croaking, hearing far voices clearly but all transmuted by evening, watching the windows in the little town glimmering one by one and seeing the gloaming dwindle solemnly into night, a great many things fell from mind that seem important by day, and evening in their place planted strange fancies.

Little winds had arisen and were whispering to and fro, it grew cold and I was about to descend the hill when I heard a voice behind me saying, "Beware, Beware."

So much the voice appeared a part of the evening that I did not turn round at first, it was like voices that one hears in sleep and thinks to be of one's dream. And the word was monotonously repeated, in French.

When I turned round I saw an old man with a horn; he had a white beard marvellously long, and still went on saying slowly, "Beware, Beware." He had clearly just come from the tower by which he stood, though I had heard no footfall. Had a man come stealthily upon me at such an hour and in so lonesome a place I had certainly felt surprised; but I saw almost at once that he was a spirit, and he seemed with his uncouth horn and his long white beard and that noiseless step of his to be so native to that time and place that I spoke to him as one does to some fellow-traveller who asks you if you mind having the window up.

I asked him what there was to beware of.

"Of what should a town beware," he said, "but the Saracens?"

"Saracens?" I said.

"Yes, Saracens. Saracens," he answered and brandished his horn.

"And who are you?" I said.

"I? I am the spirit of the tower," he said.

When I asked him how he came by so human an aspect and was so unlike the material tower beside him, he told me that the lives of all the watchers who had ever held the horn in the tower there had gone to make the spirit of the tower. "It takes a hundred lives," he said. "None hold the horn of late and men neglect the tower. When the walls are in ill repair the Saracens còme: it was ever so."

"The Saracens don't come nowadays," I said.

But he was gazing past me watching and did not seem to heed me.

"They will run down those hills," he said, pointing away to the south, "out of the woods about nightfall, and I shall blow my horn. The people will all come up from the town to the tower again; but the loopholes are in very ill repair."

"We never hear of the Saracens now," I said.

"Hear of the Saracens!" the old spirit said. "Hear of the Saracens! They slip one evening out of that forest in the long white robes that they wear, and I blow my horn. That is the first that anyone ever hears of the Saracens."

"I mean," I said, "that they never come at all. They cannot come, and men fear other things." For I thought the old spirit might rest if he knew that the Saracens can never come again. But he said, "There is nothing in the world to fear but the Saracens. Nothing else matters. How can men fear other things?"

Then I explained, so that he might have rest, and told him how all Europe, and in particular France, had terrible engines of war, both on land and on sea, and how the Saracens had not these terrible engines either on sea or land, and so could by no means cross the Mediterranean or escape destruction on shore even though they should come there. I alluded to the European railways that could move armies night and day faster than horses could gallop. And when as well as I could I had explained all, he answered, "In time all these things pass away and there will still be the Saracens."

And then I said, "There has not been a Saracen either in France or Spain for over four hundred years."

And he said, "The Saracens! You do not know their cunning. That was ever the way of the Saracens. They do not come for a while, no not they for a long while, and then one day they come."

And peering southwards, but not seeing clearly because of the rising mist, he silently moved to his tower and up its broken steps.

The Secret of the Sea

In an ill-lit ancient tavern that I know are many tales of the sea; but not without the wine of Gorgondy, that I had of a private bargain from the gnomes, was the tale laid bare for which I had waited of an evening for the greater part of a year.

I knew my man and listened to his stories, sitting amid the bluster of his oaths; I plied him with rum and whiskey and mixed drinks, but there never came the tale for which I sought, and as a last resort I went to the Huthneth Mountains and bargained there all night with the chiefs of the gnomes.

When I came to the ancient tavern and entered the low-roofed room, bringing the hoard of the gnomes in a bottle of hammered iron, my man had not yet arrived. The sailors laughed at my old iron bottle, but I sat down and waited; had I opened it then they would have wept and sung. I was well content to wait, for I knew my man had the story, and it was such a one as had profoundly stirred the incredulity of the faithless.

He entered and greeted me, and sat down and called for brandy. He was a hard man to turn from his purpose, and, uncorking my iron bottle, I sought to dissuade him from brandy for fear that when the brandy bit his throat he should refuse to leave it for any other wine. He lifted his head and said deep and dreadful things of any man that should dare to speak against brandy.

I swore that I said nothing against brandy, but added that it was often given to children, while Gorgondy was only drunk by men of such depravity that they had abandoned sin because all the usual vices had come to seem genteel. When he asked if Gorgondy was a bad wine to drink, I said that it was so bad that if a man sipped it that was the one touch that made damnation certain. Then he asked me what I had in the iron bottle, and I said it was Gorgondy; and then he shouted for the largest tumbler in that ill-lit ancient tavern, and stood up and shook his fist at me when it came, and swore, and told me to fill it with the wine that I got on that bitter night from the treasure-house of the gnomes.

As he drank it he told me that he had met men who had spoken against wine, and that they had mentioned Heaven; and therefore he would not go there—no, not he; and that once he had sent one of them to Hell, but when he got there he would turn him out, and he had no use for milksops.

Over the second tumbler he was thoughtful, but still he said no word of the tale he knew, until I feared that it would never be heard. But when the third glass of that terrific wine had burned its way down his gullet, and vindicated the wickedness of the gnomes, his reticence withered like a leaf in the fire, and he bellowed out the secret.

I had long known that there is in ships a will or way of their own, and had even suspected that when sailors die or abandon their ships at sea, a derelict, being left to her own devices, may seek her own ends; but I had never dreamed by night, or fancied during the day, that the ships had a god that they worshipped, or that they secretly slipped away to a temple in the sea.

Over the fourth glass of the wine that the gnomes so sinfully brew but have kept so wisely from man, until the bargain that I had with their elders all through that autumn night, the sailor told me the story. I do not tell it as he told it to me because of the oaths that were in it; nor is it from delicacy that I refrain from writing these oaths verbatim, but merely because the horror they caused in me at the time troubles me still whenever I put them on paper, and I continue to shudder until I have blotted them out. Therefore, I tell the story in my own words, which, if they possess a certain decency that was not in the mouth of that sailor, unfortunately do not smack, as his did, of rum and blood and the sea.

You would take a ship to be a dead thing like a table, as dead as bits of iron and canvas and wood. That is because you always live on shore, and have never seen the sea, and drink milk. Milk is a more accursed drink than water.

What with the captain and what with the man at the wheel, and what with the crew, a ship has no fair chance of showing a will of her own.

There is only one moment in the history of ships, that carry crews on board, when they act by their own free will. This moment comes when all the crew are drunk. As the last man

falls drunk on to the deck, the ship is free of man, and immediately slips away. She slips away at once on a new course and
is never one yard out in a hundred miles.

It was like this one night with the *Sea-Fancy*. Bill Smiles
was there himself, and can vouch for it. Bill Smiles has never
told this tale before for fear that anyone should call him a liar.
Nobody dislikes being hung as much as Bill Smiles would, but
he won't be called a liar. I tell the tale as I heard it, relevancies
and irrelevancies, though in my more decent words; and as I
made no doubts of the truth of it then, I hardly like to now;
others can please themselves.

It is not often that the whole of a crew is drunk. The crew of
the *Sea-Fancy* was no drunkener than others. It happened like
this.

The captain was always drunk. One day a fancy he had that
some spiders were plotting against him, or a sudden bleeding
he had from both his ears, made him think that drinking
might be bad for his health. Next day he signed the pledge. He
was sober all that morning and all the afternoon, but at
evening he saw a sailor drinking a glass of beer, and a fit of
madness seized him, and he said things that seemed bad to
Bill Smiles. And next morning he made all of them take the
pledge.

For two days nobody had a drop to drink, unless you count
water, and on the third morning the captain was quite drunk.
It stood to reason they all had a glass or two then, except the
man at the wheel; and towards evening the man at the wheel
could bear it no longer, and seems to have had his glass like all
the rest, for the ship's course wobbled a bit and made a circle or
two. Then all of a sudden she went off south by east under full
canvas till midnight, and never altered her course. And at midnight she came to the wide wet courts of the Temple in the Sea.

People who think that Mr. Smiles is drunk often make a
great mistake. And people are not the only ones that have
made that mistake. Once a ship made it, and a lot of ships. It's
a mistake to think that old Bill Smiles is drunk just because
he can't move.

Midnight and moonlight and the Temple in the Sea Bill
Smiles clearly remembers, and all the derelicts in the world
were there, the old abandoned ships. The figureheads were
nodding to themselves and blinking at the image. The image
was a woman of white marble on a pedestal in the outer court

of the Temple of the Sea: she was clearly the love of all the man-deserted ships, or the goddess to whom they prayed their heathen prayers. And as Bill Smiles was watching them, the lips of the figureheads moved; they all began to pray. But all at once their lips were closed with a snap when they saw that there were men on the *Sea-Fancy*. They all came crowding up and nodded and nodded and nodded to see if all were drunk, and that's when they made their mistake about old Bill Smiles, although he couldn't move. They would have given up the treasuries of the gulfs sooner than let men hear the prayers they said or guess their love for the goddess. It is the intimate secret of the sea.

The sailor paused. And, in my eagerness to hear what lyrical or blasphemous thing those figureheads prayed by moonlight at midnight in the sea to the woman of marble who was a goddess to ships, I pressed on the sailor more of my Gorgondy wine that the gnomes so wickedly brew.

I should never have done it; but there he was sitting silent while the secret was almost mine. He took it moodily and drank a glass; and with the other glasses that he had had he fell a prey to the villainy of the gnomes who brew this unbridled wine to no good end. His body leaned forward slowly, then fell on to the table, his face being sideways and full of a wicked smile, and, saying very clearly the one word, "Hell," he became silent for ever with the secret he had from the sea.

How Plash-Goo Came
to the Land of None's Desire

In a thatched cottage of enormous size, so vast that we might consider it a palace, but only a cottage in the style of its building, its timbers and the nature of its interior, there lived Plash-Goo.

Plash-Goo was of the children of the giants, whose sire was Uph. And the lineage of Uph had dwindled in bulk for the last five hundred years, till the giants were now no more than fifteen feet high; but Uph ate elephants which he caught with his hands.

Now on the tops of the mountains above the house of Plash-Goo, for Plash-Goo lived in the plains, there dwelt the dwarf whose name was Lrippity-Kang.

And the dwarf used to walk at evening on the edge of the tops of the mountains, and would walk up and down along it, and was squat and ugly and hairy, and was plainly seen of Plash-Goo.

And for many weeks the giant had suffered the sight of him, but at length grew irked at the sight (as men are by little things) and could not sleep of a night and lost his taste for pigs. And at last there came the day, as anyone might have known, when Plash-Goo shouldered his club and went up to look for the dwarf.

And the dwarf though briefly squat was broader than may be dreamed, beyond all breadth of man, and stronger than men may know; strength in its very essence dwelt in that little frame, as a spark in the heart of a flint: but to Plash-Goo he was no more than misshapen, bearded and squat, a thing that dared to defy all natural laws by being more broad than long.

When Plash-Goo came to the mountain he cast his chima-halk down (for so he named the club of his heart's desire) lest the dwarf should defy him with nimbleness; and stepped towards Lrippity-Kang with gripping hands, who stopped in his mountainous walk without a word, and swung round his hideous breadth to confront Plash-Goo.

Already then Plash-Goo in the deeps of his mind had seen himself seize the dwarf in one large hand and hurl him with his beard and his hated breadth sheer down the precipice that dropped away from that very place to the Land of None's Desire. Yet it was otherwise that Fate would have it. For the dwarf parried with his little arms the grip of those monstrous hands, and gradually working along the enormous limbs came at length to the giant's body where by dwarfish cunning he obtained a grip; and turning Plash-Goo about, as a spider does some great fly, till his little grip was suitable to his purpose, he suddenly lifted the giant over his head. Slowly at first, by the edge of that precipice whose base sheer distance hid, he swung his giant victim round his head, but soon faster and faster; and at last when Plash-Goo was streaming round the hated breadth of the dwarf and the no less hated beard was flapping in the wind, Lrippity-Kang let go. Plash-Goo shot over the edge and for some way further, out towards Space, like a stone; then he began to fall. It was long before he believed and truly knew that this was really he that fell from this mountain, for we do not associate such dooms with ourselves; but when he had fallen for some while through the evening and saw below him, where there had been nothing to see, or *began* to see, the glimmer of tiny fields, then his optimism departed; till later on when the fields were greener and larger he saw that this was indeed (and growing how terribly nearer) that very land to which he had destined the dwarf.

At last he saw it unmistakable, close, with its grim houses and its dreadful ways, and its green fields shining in the light of the evening. His cloak was streaming from him in whistling shreds.

So Plash-Goo came to the Land of None's Desire.

The Three Sailors' Gambit

Sitting some years ago in the ancient tavern at Over, one afternoon in spring, I was waiting as was my custom for something strange to happen.

In this I was not always disappointed, for the very curious leaded panes of that tavern, facing the sea, let a light into the low-ceilinged room so mysterious, particularly at evening, that it somehow seemed to affect the events within. Be that as it may, I have seen strange things in that tavern and heard stranger things told.

And as I sat there three sailors entered the tavern just back, as they said, from sea and come with sun-burned skins from a very long voyage to the South; and one of them had a board and chessmen under his arm, and they were complaining that they could find no one who knew how to play chess. This was the year that the Tournament was in England. And a little dark man at a table in a corner of the room, drinking sugar and water, asked them why they wished to play chess; and they said that they would play any man for a pound. They opened their box of chessmen then, a cheap and nasty set, and the man refused to play with such uncouth pieces, and the sailors suggested that perhaps he could find better ones; and in the end he went round to his lodgings near by and brought his own, and then they sat down to play for a pound a side. It was a consultation game on the part of the sailors, they said all three must play.

Well, the little dark man turned out to be Stavlokratz.

Of course he was fabulously poor, and the sovereign meant more to him than it did to the sailors, but he didn't seem keen to play, it was the sailors that insisted; he had made the badness of the sailors' chessmen an excuse for not playing at all, but the sailors had overruled that, and then he told them straight out who he was, and the sailors had never heard of Stavlokratz.

Well, no more was said after that. Stavlokratz said no more,

136

either because he did not wish to boast or because he was
huffed that they did not know who he was. And I saw no reason to enlighten the sailors about him; if he took their pound
they had brought it on themselves, and my boundless admira-
tion for his genius made me feel that he deserved whatever
might come his way. He had not asked to play, they had named
the stakes, he had warned them, and gave them first move;
there was nothing unfair about Stavlokratz.

I had never seen Stavlokratz before, but I had played over
nearly every one of his games in the World Championship for
the last three or four years; he was always, of course, the
model chosen by students. Only young chess-players can
appreciate my delight at seeing him play first hand.

Well, the sailors used to lower their heads almost as low as
the table and mutter together before every move, but they
muttered so low that you could not hear what they planned.

They lost three pawns almost straight off, then a knight, and
shortly after a bishop; they were playing in fact the famous
Three Sailors' Gambit.

Stavlokratz was playing with the easy confidence that they
say was usual with him, when suddenly at about the thir-
teenth move I saw him look surprised; he leaned forward and
looked at the board and then at the sailors, but he learned
nothing from their vacant faces; he looked back at the board
again.

He moved more deliberately after that; the sailors lost two
more pawns, Stavlokratz had lost nothing as yet. He looked at
me, I thought, almost irritably, as though something would
happen that he wished I was not there to see. I believed at first
he had qualms about taking the sailors' pound, until it dawned
on me that he might lose the game; I saw that possibility in his
face, not on the board, for the game had become almost incom-
prehensible to me. I cannot describe my astonishment. And a
few moves later Stavlokratz resigned.

The sailors showed no more elation than if they had won
some game with greasy cards, playing amongst themselves.

Stavlokratz asked them where they got their opening. "We
kind of thought of it," said one. "It just come into our heads
like," said another. He asked them questions about the ports
they had touched at. He evidently thought, as I did myself,
that they had learned their extraordinary gambit, perhaps in
some old dependency of Spain, from some young master of

chess whose fame had not reached Europe. He was very eager
to find who this man could be, for neither of us imagined that
those sailors had invented it, nor would anyone who had seen
them. But he got no information from the sailors.

Stavlokratz could very ill afford the loss of a pound. He
offered to play them again for the same stakes. The sailors
began to set up the white pieces. Stavlokratz pointed out that
it was his turn for first move. The sailors agreed but continued
to set up the white pieces and sat with the white before them
waiting for him to move. It was a trivial incident, but it
revealed to Stavlokratz and myself that none of these sailors
was aware that white always moves first.

Stavlokratz played on them his own opening, reasoning of
course that as they had never heard of Stavlokratz they would
not know of his opening; and with probably a very good hope of
getting back his pound he played the fifth variation with its
tricky seventh move, at least so he intended, but it turned to a
variation unknown to the students of Stavlokratz.

Throughout this game I watched the sailors closely, and I
became sure, as only an attentive watcher can be, that the one
on their left, Jim Bunion, did not even know the moves.

When I had made up my mind about this I watched only the
other two, Adam Bailey and Bill Sloggs, trying to make out
which was the master mind; and for a long while I could not.
And then I heard Adam Bailey mutter six words, the only
words I heard throughout the game, of all their consultations,
"No, him with the horse's head." And I decided that Adam
Bailey did not know what a knight was, though of course he
might have been explaining things to Bill Sloggs, but it did not
sound like that; so that left Bill Sloggs. I watched Bill Sloggs
after that with a certain wonder; he was no more intellectual
than the others to look at, though rather more forceful perhaps. Poor old Stavlokratz was beaten again.

Well, in the end I paid for Stavlokratz, and tried to get a
game with Bill Sloggs alone; but this he would not agree to, it
must be all three or none. And then I went back with
Stavlokratz to his lodgings. He very kindly gave me a game: of
course it did not last long, but I am more proud of having been
beaten by Stavlokratz than of any game that I have ever won.
And then we talked for an hour about the sailors, and neither
of us could make head or tale of them. I told him what I had
noticed about Jim Bunion and Adam Bailey, and he agreed

with me that Bill Sloggs was the man, though as to how he had
come by that gambit or that variation of Stavlokratz's own
opening he had no theory.

I had the sailors' address, which was that tavern as much as
anywhere, and they were to be there all that evening. As
evening drew in I went back to the tavern, and found there
still the three sailors. And I offered Bill Sloggs two pounds for
a game with him alone and he refused, but in the end he
played me for a drink. And then I found that he had not heard
of the *en passant* rule, and believed that the fact of checking
the king prevented him from castling, and did not know that a
player can have two or more queens on the board at the same
time if he queens his pawns, or that a pawn could ever become
a knight; and he made as many of the stock mistakes as he had
time for in a short game, which I won. I thought that I should
have got at the secret then, but his mates who had sat scowling all the while in the corner came up and interfered. It was
a breach of their compact apparently for one to play chess by
himself; at any rate they seemed angry. So I left the tavern
then and came back again next day, and the next day and the
day after, and often saw the three sailors, but none were in a
communicative mood. I had got Stavlokratz to keep away, and
they could get no one to play chess with at a pound a side, and
I would not play with them unless they told me the secret.

And then one evening I found Jim Bunion drunk, yet not so
drunk as he wished, for the two pounds were spent; and I gave
him very nearly a tumbler of whiskey, or what passed for
whiskey in that tavern in Over, and he told me the secret at
once. I had given the others some whiskey to keep them quiet,
and later on in the evening they must have gone out, but Jim
Bunion stayed with me by a little table, leaning across it and
talking low, right into my face, his breath smelling all the
while of what passed for whiskey.

The wind was blowing outside as it does on bad nights in
November, coming up with moans from the south, towards
which the tavern faced with all its leaded panes, so that none
but I was able to hear his voice as Jim Bunion gave up his
secret.

They had sailed for years, he told me, with Bill Snyth; and
on their last voyage home Bill Snyth had died. And he was
buried at sea. Just the other side of the line they buried him,
and his pals divided his kit, and these three got his crystal that

only they knew he had, which Bill got one night in Cuba. They played chess with the crystal.

And he was going on to tell me about that night in Cuba when Bill had bought the crystal from the stranger, how some folks might think that they had seen thunderstorms, but let them go and listen to that one that thundered in Cuba when Bill was buying his crystal and they'd find that they didn't know what thunder was. But then I interrupted him, unfortunately perhaps, for it broke the thread of his tale and set him rambling awhile, and cursing other people and talking of other lands, China, Port Said and Spain: but I brought him back to Cuba again in the end. I asked him how they could play chess with a crystal; and he said that you looked at the board and looked at the crystal and there was the game in the crystal the same as it was on the board, with all the odd little pieces looking just the same though smaller, horses' heads and whatnots; and as soon as the other man moved the move came out in the crystal, and then your move appeared after it, and all you had to do was to make it on the board. If you didn't make the move that you saw in the crystal things got very bad in it, everything horribly mixed and moving about rapidly, and scowling and making the same move over and over again, and the crystal getting cloudier and cloudier; it was best to take one's eyes away from it then, or one dreamt about it afterwards, and the foul little pieces came and cursed you in your sleep and moved about all night with their crooked moves.

I thought then that, drunk though he was, he was not telling the truth, and I promised to show him to people who played chess all their lives so that he and his mates could get a pound whenever they liked, and I promised not to reveal his secret even to Stavlokratz, if only he would tell me all the truth; and this promise I have kept till long after the three sailors have lost their secret. I told him straight out that I did not believe in the crystal. Well, Jim Bunion leaned forward then, even further across the table, and swore he had seen the man from whom Bill had bought the crystal and that he was one to whom anything was possible. To begin with, his hair was villainously dark, and his features were unmistakable even down there in the South, and he could play chess with his eyes shut, and even then he could beat anyone in Cuba. But there was more than this, there was the bargain he made with Bill that told one who he was. He sold that crystal for Bill Snyth's soul.

Jim Bunion, leaning over the table with his breath in my face, nodded his head several times and was silent.

I began to question him then. Did they play chess as far away as Cuba? He said they all did. Was it conceivable that any man would make such a bargain as Snyth made? Wasn't the trick well known? Wasn't it in hundreds of books? And if he couldn't read books, mustn't he have heard from sailors that that is the Devil's commonest dodge to get souls from silly people?

Jim Bunion had leant back in his own chair quietly smiling at my questions, but when I mentioned silly people he leaned forward again, and thrust his face close to mine and asked me several times if I called Bill Snyth silly. It seemed that these three sailors thought a great deal of Bill Snyth, and it made Jim Bunion angry to hear anything said against him. I hastened to say that the bargain seemed silly, though not, of course, the man who made it; for the sailor was almost threatening, and no wonder, for the whiskey in that dim tavern would madden a nun.

When I said that the bargain seemed silly he smiled again, and then he thundered his fist down on the table and said that no one had ever got the better of Bill Snyth, and that that was the worst bargain for himself that the Devil ever made, and that from all he had read or heard of the Devil he had never been so badly had before as the night when he met Bill Snyth at the inn in the thunderstorm in Cuba, for Bill Snyth already had the damndest soul at sea; Bill was a good fellow, but his soul was damned right enough, so he got the crystal for nothing.

Yes, he was there and saw it all himself, Bill Snyth in the Spanish inn and the candles flaring, and the Devil walking in out of the rain, and then the bargain between those two old hands, and the Devil going out into the lightning, and the thunderstorm raging on, and Bill Snyth sitting chuckling to himself between the bursts of the thunder.

But I had more questions to ask and interrupted this reminiscence. Why did they all three always play together? And a look of something like fear came over Jim Bunion's face; and at first he would not speak. And then he said to me that it was like this; they had not paid for that crystal, but got it as their share of Bill Snyth's kit. If they had paid for it or given something in exchange to Bill Snyth that would have been all right, but they couldn't do that now because Bill was dead, and they were not sure if the old bargain might not hold good. And Hell must be a large and lonely place, and to go there alone must be bad; and so the three agreed that they would all stick together, and use the crystal all three or not at all, unless one died, and then the two would use it and the one that was gone would wait for them. And the last of the three to go would bring the crystal with him, or maybe the crystal would bring him. They didn't think, he said, they were the kind of men for Heaven, and he hoped they knew their place better than that, but they didn't fancy the notion of Hell alone, if Hell it had to be. It was all right for Bill Snyth, he was afraid of nothing. He had known perhaps five men that were not afraid of death, but Bill Snyth was not afraid of Hell. He died with a smile on his face like a child in its sleep; it was drink killed poor Bill Snyth.

This was why I had beaten Bill Sloggs; Sloggs had the crystal on him while we played, but would not use it; these sailors seemed to fear loneliness as some people fear being hurt; he was the only one of the three who could play chess at all, he had learnt it in order to be able to answer questions and keep up their pretence, but he had learnt it badly, as I found. I never saw the crystal, they never showed it to anyone; but Jim Bunion told me that night that it was about the size that the thick end of a hen's egg would be if it were round. And then he fell asleep.

There were many more questions that I would have asked him but I could not wake him up. I even pulled the table away so that he fell to the floor, but he slept on, and all the tavern was dark but for one candle burning; and it was then that I noticed for the first time that the other two sailors had gone; no one remained at all but Jim Bunion and I and the sinister barman of that curious inn, and he too was asleep.

When I saw that it was impossible to wake the sailor I went out into the night. Next day Jim Bunion would talk of it no more; and when I went back to Stavlokratz I found him already putting on paper his theory about the sailors, which became accepted by chess-players, that one of them had been taught their curious gambit and the other two between them had learnt all the defensive openings as well as general play. Though who taught them no one could say, in spite of enquiries made afterwards all along the Southern Pacific.

I never learnt any more details from any of the three sailors, they were always too drunk to speak or else not drunk enough to be communicative. I seem just to have taken Jim Bunion at the flood. But I kept my promise; it was I that introduced them to the Tournament, and a pretty mess they made of established reputations. And so they kept on for months, never losing a game and always playing for their pound a side. I used to follow them wherever they went merely to watch their play. They were more marvellous than Stavlokratz even in his youth.

But then they took to liberties such as giving their queen when playing first-class players. And in the end one day when all three were drunk they played the best player in England with only a row of pawns. They won the game all right. But the ball broke to pieces. I never smelt such a stench in all my life.

The three sailors took it stoically enough, they signed on to different ships and went back again to the sea, and the world of chess lost sight, for ever I trust, of the most remarkable players it ever knew, who would have altogether spoiled the game.

How Ali Came to
the Black Country

Shooshan the barber went to Shep the maker of teeth to discuss the state of England. They agreed that it was time to send for Ali.

So Shooshan stepped late that night from the little shop near Fleet Street and made his way back again to his house in the ends of London and sent at once the message that brought Ali.

And Ali came, mostly on foot, from the country of Persia, and it took him a year to come; but when he came he was welcome.

And Shep told Ali what was the matter with England, and Shooshan swore that it was so, and Ali looking out of the window of the little shop near Fleet Street beheld the ways of London and audibly blessed King Solomon and his seal.

When Shep and Shooshan heard the names of King Solomon and his seal both asked, as they had scarcely dared before, if Ali had it. Ali patted a little bundle of silks that he drew from his inner raiment. It was there.

Now concerning the movements and courses of the stars, and the influence on them of spirits of Earth and devils, this age has been rightly named by some The Second Age of Ignorance. But Ali knew. And by watching nightly, for seven nights in Bagdad, the way of certain stars he had found out the dwelling-place of Him They Needed.

Guided by Ali all three set forth for the Midlands. And by the reverence that was manifest in the faces of Shep and Shooshan towards the person of Ali, some knew what Ali carried, while others said that it was the tablets of the Law, others the name of God, and others that he must have a lot of money about him. So they passed Slod and Apton.

And at last they came to the town for which Ali sought, that spot over which he had seen the shy stars wheel and swerve away from their orbits, being troubled. Verily when they came there were no stars, though it was midnight. And Ali said that it was the appointed place. In harems in Persia in the evening, when the tales go round, it is still told how Ali and Shep and Shooshan came to the Black Country.

When it was dawn they looked upon the country and saw how it was without doubt the appointed place, even as Ali had said; for the earth had been taken out of pits and burned and left lying in heaps, and there were many factories, and they stood over the town and as it were rejoiced. And with one voice Shep and Shooshan gave praise to Ali.

And Ali said that the great ones of the place must needs be gathered together, and to this end Shep and Shooshan went into the town and there spoke craftily. For they said that Ali had of his wisdom contrived as it were a patent and a novelty, which should greatly benefit England. And when they heard how he sought nothing for his novelty save only to benefit mankind they consented to speak with Ali and see his novelty. And they came forth and met Ali.

And Ali spake and said unto them, "O lords of this place; in the book that all men know it is written how that a fisherman casting his net into the sea drew up a bottle of brass, and when he took the stopper from the bottle a dreadful genie of horrible aspect rose from the bottle, as it were like a smoke, even to darkening the sky, whereat the fisherman . . ." And the great ones of that place said, "We have heard the story." And Ali said, "What became of that genie after he was safely thrown back into the sea is not properly spoken of by any save those that pursue the study of demons, and not with certainty by any man; but that the stopper that bore the ineffable seal, and bears it to this day, became separate from the bottle, is among those things that man may know." And when there was doubt among the great ones Ali drew forth his bundle and one by one removed those many silks till the seal stood revealed; and some of them knew it for the seal and others knew it not.

And they looked curiously at it and listened to Ali, and Ali said:

"Having heard how evil is the case of England, how a smoke has darkened the country, and in places (as men say) the grass is black, and how even yet your factories multiply, and haste and noise have become such that men have no time for song, I have therefore come at the bidding of my good friend Shooshan, barber of London, and of Shep, a maker of teeth, to make things well with you."

And they said: "But where is your patent and your novelty?"

And Ali said: "Have I not here the stopper and on it, as good men know, the ineffable seal? Now I have learned in Persia how that your trains that make the haste, and hurry men to and fro, and your factories and the digging of your pits, and all the things that are evil, are every one of them caused and brought about by steam."

"Is it not so?" said Shooshan.

"It is even so," said Shep.

"Now it is clear," said Ali, "that the chief devil that vexes England and has done all this harm, who herds men into cities and will not let them rest, is even the devil Steam."

Then the great ones would have rebuked him but one said: "No, let us hear him, perhaps his patent may improve on steam."

And to them hearkening Ali went on thus: "O Lords of this place, let there be made a bottle of strong steel, for I have no bottle with my stopper, and this being done let all the factories, trains, digging of pits, and all evil things soever that may be done by steam, be stopped for seven days, and the men that tend them shall go free, but the steel bottle for my stopper I will leave open in a likely place. Now that chief devil, Steam, finding no factories to enter into, nor no trains, sirens nor pits prepared for him, and, being curious and accustomed to steel pots, will verily enter one night into the bottle that you shall make for my stopper, and I shall spring forth from my hiding with my stopper and fasten him down with the ineffable seal, which is the seal of King Solomon, and deliver him up to you that you cast him into the sea."

And the great ones answered Ali and they said: "But what should we gain if we lose our prosperity and be no longer rich?"

And Ali said: "When we have cast this devil into the sea there will come back again the woods and ferns and all the beautiful things that the world hath, the little leaping hares shall be seen at play, there shall be music on the hills again, and at twilight ease and quiet, and after the twilight stars."

And "Verily," said Shooshan, "there shall be the dance again."

"Aye," said Shep, "there shall be the country dance."

But the great ones spake and said, denying Ali: "We will make no such bottle for your stopper nor stop our healthy factories or good trains, nor cease from our digging of pits nor do

anything that you desire, for an interference with steam would
strike at the roots of that prosperity that you see so plentifully
all around us."

Thus they dismissed Ali there and then from that place
where the earth was torn up and burnt, being taken out of pits,
and where factories blazed all night with a demoniac glare;
and they dismissed with him both Shooshan, the barber, and
Shep, the maker of teeth: so that a week later Ali started from
Calais on his long walk back to Persia.

And all this happened thirty years ago, and Shep is an old
man now and Shooshan older, and many mouths have bit with
the teeth of Shep (for he has a knack of getting them back
whenever his customers die), and they have written again to
Ali away in the country of Persia with these words, saying:

"O Ali. The devil has indeed begotten a devil, even that spirit
Petrol. And the young devil waxeth, and increaseth in lusti-
hood and is ten years old and becoming like to his father. Come
therefore and help us with the ineffable seal. For there is none
like Ali."

And Ali turns where his slaves scatter rose-leaves, letting
the letter fall, and deeply draws from his hookah a puff of the
scented smoke, right down into his lungs, and sighs it forth
and smiles, and lolling round on to his other elbow speaks com-
fortably and says, "And shall a man go twice to the help of a
dog?"

And with these words he thinks no more of England but pon-
ders again the inscrutable ways of God.

The Exiles' Club

It was an evening party; and something someone had said to me had started me talking about a subject that to me is full of fascination, the subject of old religions, forsaken gods. The truth (for all religions have some of it), the wisdom, the beauty, of the religions of countries to which I travel have not the same appeal for me; for one only notices in them their tyranny and intolerance and the abject servitude that they claim from thought; but when a dynasty has been dethroned in heaven and goes forgotten and outcast even among men, one's eyes no longer dazzled by its power find something very wistful in the faces of fallen gods suppliant to be remembered, something almost tearfully beautiful, like a long warm summer twilight fading gently away after some day memorable in the story of earthly wars. Between what Zeus, for instance, has been once and the half-remembered tale he is to-day there lies a space so great that there is no change of fortune known to man whereby we may measure the height down which he has fallen. And it is the same with many another god at whom once the ages trembled and the twentieth century treats as an old wives' tale. The fortitude that such a fall demands is surely more than human.

Some such things as these I was saying, and being upon a subject that much attracts me I possibly spoke too loudly. Certainly I was not aware that standing close behind me was no less a person than the ex-King of Eritivaria, the thirty islands of the East, or I wold have moderated my voice and moved away a little to give him more room. I was not aware of his presence until his satellite, one who had fallen with him into exile but still revolved about him, told me that his master desired to know me: and so to my surprise I was presented, though neither of them even knew my name. And that was how I came to be invited by the ex-King to dine at his club.

At the time I could only account for his wishing to know me by supposing that he found in his own exiled condition some likeliness to the fallen fortunes of the gods of whom I talked unwitting of his presence; but now I know that it was not of himself he was thinking when he asked me to dine at that club.

The club would have been the most imposing building in any street in London, but in that obscure mean quarter of London in which they had built it it appeared unduly enormous. Lifting right up above those grotesque houses, and built in that Greek style that we call Georgian, there was something Olympian about it. To my host an unfashionable street could have meant nothing, through all his youth wherever he had gone had become fashionable the moment he went there: words like the East End could have had no meaning to him.

Whoever built that house had enormous wealth and cared nothing for fashion, perhaps despised it. As I stood gazing at the magnificent upper windows draped with great curtains, indistinct in the evening, on which huge shadows flickered, my host attracted my attention from the doorway, and so I went in and met for the second time the ex-King of Eritivaria.

In front of us a stairway of rare marble led upwards. He took me through a side-door and downstairs and we came to a banqueting-hall of great magnificence. A long table ran up the middle of it, laid for quite twenty people, and I noticed the peculiarity that instead of chairs there were thrones, for everyone except me, who was the only guest and for whom there was an ordinary chair. My host explained to me when we all sat down that everyone who belonged to that club was by rights a king.

In fact none was permitted, he told me, to belong to the club until his claim to a kingdom, made out in writing, had been examined and allowed by those whose duty it was. The whim of a populace or the candidate's own misrule were never considered by the investigators, nothing counted with them but heredity and lawful descent from kings, all else was ignored. At that table there were those who had once reigned themselves, others lawfully claimed descent from kings that the world had forgotten, the kingdoms claimed by some had even changed their names. Hatzgurh, the mountain Kingdom, is almost regarded as mythical.

I have seldom seen greater splendour than that long hall provided below the level of the street. No doubt by day it was a little sombre, as all basements are, but at night with its great crystal chandeliers, and the glitter of heirlooms that had gone into exile, it surpassed the splendour of palaces that have

only one king. They had come to London suddenly, most of
those kings, or their fathers before them or forefathers; some
had come away from their kingdoms by night, in a light sleigh,
flogging the horses, or had galloped clear with morning over
the border; some had trudged roads for days from their capital
in disguise, yet many had had time just as they left to snatch
up some small thing without price in markets, for the sake of
old times as they said, but quite as much, I thought, with an
eye to the future. And there these treasures glittered on that
long table in the banqueting-hall of the basement of that
strange club. Merely to see them was much, but to hear their
story that their owners told was to go back in fancy to epic
times on the romantic border of fable and fact, where the
heroes of history fought with the gods of myth. The famous silver horses of Gilgianza were there, climbing their sheer mountain, which they did by miraculous means before the time of
the Goths. It was not a large piece of silver, but its workman-
ship out-rivalled the skill of the bees.

A yellow Emperor had brought out of the East a piece of that
incomparable porcelain that had made his dynasty famous
though all their deeds are forgotten, it had the exact shade of
the right purple.

And there was a little golden statuette of a dragon stealing
a diamond from a lady, the dragon had the diamond in his
claws, large and of the first water. There had been a kingdom
whose whole constitution and history were founded on the legend, from which alone its kings had claimed their right to the
sceptre, that a dragon stole a diamond from a lady. When its
last king left that country, because his favourite general used
a peculiar formation under the fire of artillery, he brought with
him the little ancient image that no longer proved him a king
outside that singular club.

There was the pair of amethyst cups of the turbaned King of
Foo, the one that he drank from himself, and the one that he
gave to his enemies: eye could not tell which was which.

All these things the ex-King of Eritivaria showed me, telling
me a marvellous tale of each; of his own he had brought nothing, except the mascot that used once to sit on the top of the
water tube of his favourite motor.

I have not outlined a tenth of the splendour of that table, I
had meant to come again and examine each piece of plate and
make notes of its history; had I known that this was the last

time I should wish to enter that club I should have looked at its treasures more attentively, but now as the wine went round and the exiles began to talk I took my eyes from the table and listened to strange tales of their former state.

He that has seen better times has usually a poor tale to tell, some mean and trivial thing has been his undoing, but they that dined in that basement had mostly fallen like oaks on nights of abnormal tempest, had fallen mightily and shaken a nation. Those who had not been kings themselves, but claimed through an exiled ancestor, had stories to tell of even grander disaster, history seeming to have mellowed their dynasty's fate as moss grows over an oak a great while fallen. There were no jealousies there as so often there are among kings, rivalry must have ceased with the loss of their navies and armies, and they showed no bitterness against those that had turned them out, one speaking of the error of his Prime Minister by which he had lost his throne as "poor old Friedrich's heaven-sent gift of tactlessness."

They gossiped pleasantly of many things, the tittle-tattle we all had to know when we were learning history, and many a wonderful story I might have heard, many a sidelight on mysterious wars, had I not made use of one unfortunate word. That word was "upstairs."

The ex-King of Eritivaria having pointed out to me those unparalleled heirlooms to which I have alluded, and many more besides, hospitably asked me if there was anything else that I would care to see; he meant the pieces of plate that they had in the cupboards, the curiously graven swords of other princes, historic jewels, legendary seals; but I who had had a glimpse of their marvellous staircase, whose balustrade I believed to be solid gold, and wondering why in such a stately house they chose to dine in the basement, mentioned the word "upstairs." A hush as at sacrilege came down on the whole assembly, the hush that might greet levity in a cathedral.

"Upstairs!" he gasped. "We cannot go upstairs."

I perceived that what I had said was an ill-chosen thing. I tried to excuse myself but knew not how.

"Of course," I muttered, "members may not take guests upstairs."

"Members!" he said to me. "We are not the members!"

There was such reproof in his voice that I said no more, I looked at him questioningly, perhaps my lips moved, I may have said, "What are you?" A great surprise had come on me at their attitude.

"We are the waiters," he said.

That I could not have known, here at least was honest ignorance that I had no need to be ashamed of, the very opulence of their table denied it.

"Then who are the members?" I asked.

Such a hush fell at that question, such a hush of genuine awe, that all of a sudden a wild thought entered my head, a thought strange and fantastic and terrible. I gripped my host by the wrist and hushed my voice.

"Are they too exiles?" I asked.

Twice as he looked in my face he gravely nodded his head.

I left that club very swiftly indeed, never to see it again, scarcely pausing to say farewell to those menial kings, and as I left the door a great window opened far up at the top of the house and a flash of lightning streamed from it and killed a dog.

The Three Infernal Jokes

This is the story that the desolate man told to me on the lonely Highland road one autumn evening with winter coming on and the stags roaring.

The saddening twilight, the mountain already black, the dreadful melancholy of the stags' voices, his friendless mournful face, all seemed to be of some most sorrowful play staged in that valley by an outcast god, a lonely play of which the hills were part and he the only actor.

For long we watched each other drawing out of the solitudes of those forsaken spaces. Then when we met he spoke.

"I will tell you a thing that will make you die of laughter. I will keep it to myself no longer. But first I must tell you how I came by it."

I do not give the story in his words with all his woeful interjections and the misery of his frantic self-reproaches, for I would not convey unnecessarily to my readers that atmosphere of sadness that was about all he said and that seemed to go with him wherever he moved.

It seems that he had been a member of a club, a West End club he called it, a respectable but quite inferior affair, probably in the City: agents belonged to it, fire insurance mostly, but life insurance and motor-agents too, it was, in fact, a touts' club.

It seems that a few of them one evening, forgetting for a moment their encyclopædias and non-stop tyres, were talking loudly over a card-table when the game had ended about their personal virtues, and a very little man with waxed moustaches who disliked the taste of wine was boasting heartily of his temperance. It was then that he who told this mournful story, drawn on by the boasts of others, leaned forward a little over the green baize into the light of the two guttering candles and revealed, no doubt a little shyly, his own extraordinary virtue. One woman was to him as ugly as another.

And the silenced boasters rose and went home to bed leaving him all alone, as he supposed, with his unequalled virtue.

And yet he was not alone, for when the rest had gone there arose a member out of a deep arm-chair at the dark end of the room and walked across to him, a man whose occupation he did not know and only now suspects.

"You have," said the stranger, "a surpassing virtue."

"I have no possible use for it," my poor friend replied.

"Then doubtless you would sell it cheap," said the stranger.

Something in the man's manner or appearance made the desolate teller of this mournful tale feel his own inferiority, which probably made him feel acutely shy, so that his mind abased itself as an Oriental does his body in the presence of a superior, or perhaps he was sleepy, or merely a little drunk. Whatever it was he only mumbled "Oh yes," instead of contradicting so mad a remark. And the stranger led the way to the room where the telephone was.

"I think you will find my firm will give a good price for it," he said; and without more ado he began with a pair of pincers to cut the wire of the telephone and the receiver. The old waiter who looked after the club they had left shuffling round the other room putting things away for the night.

"Whatever are you doing of?" said my friend.

"This way," said the stranger. Along a passage they went and away to the back of the club, and there the stranger leaned out of a window and fastened the severed wires to the lightning conductor. My friend has no doubt of that, a broad ribbon of copper, half an inch wide, perhaps wider, running down from the roof to the earth.

"Hell," said the stranger with his mouth to the telephone; then silence for a while with his ear to the receiver, leaning out of the window. And then my friend heard his poor virtue being several times repeated, and then words like Yes and No.

"They offer you three jokes," said the stranger, "which shall make all who hear them simply die of laughter."

I think my friend was reluctant then to have anything more to do with it, he wanted to go home; he said he didn't want jokes.

"They think very highly of your virtue," said the stranger. And at that, odd as it seems, my friend wavered, for logically if they thought highly of the goods they should have paid a higher price.

"O all right," he said.

The extraordinary document that the agent drew from his pocket ran something like this:

"I . . . in consideration of three new jokes received from Mr. Montagu-Montague, hereinafter to be called the agent, and warranted to be as by him stated and described, do assign to him, yield, abrogate and give up, all recognitions, emoluments, perquisites or rewards due to me Here or Elsewhere on account of the following virtue, to wit and that is to say . . . that all women are to me equally ugly." The last eight words being filled in in ink by Mr. Montagu-Montague.

My poor friend duly signed it. "These are the jokes," said the agent. They were boldly written on three slips of paper. "They don't seem very funny," said the other when he had read them. "You are immune," said Mr. Montagu-Montague, "but anyone else who hears them will simply die of laughter: that we guarantee."

An American firm had bought at the price of waste paper a hundred thousand copies of *The Dictionary of Electricity,* written when electricity was new—and it had turned out that even at the time its author had not rightly grasped his subject,—the firm had paid £10,000 to a respectable English paper (no other in fact than the Briton) for the use of its name, and to obtain orders for *The Briton Dictionary of Electricity* was the occupation of my unfortunate friend. He seems to have had a way with him. Apparently he knew by a glance at a man, or a look round at his garden, whether to recommend the book as "an absolutely up-to-date achievement, the finest thing of its kind in the world of modern science" or as "at once quaint and imperfect, a thing to buy and to keep as a tribute to those dear old times that are gone." So he went on with this quaint though usual business, putting aside the memory of that night as an occasion on which he had "somewhat exceeded" as they say in circles where a spade is called neither a spade nor an agricultural implement, but is never mentioned at all, being altogether too vulgar.

And then one night he put on his suit of dress clothes and found the three jokes in the pocket. That was perhaps a shock. He seems to have thought it over carefully then, and the end of it was he gave a dinner at the club to twenty of the members. The dinner would do no harm he thought—might even help the business, and if the joke came off he would be a witty fellow, and two jokes still up his sleeve.

Whom he invited or how the dinner went I do not know, for he began to speak rapidly and came straight to the point, as a

stick that nears a cataract suddenly goes faster and faster. The
dinner was duly served, the port went round, the twenty men
were smoking, two waiters loitered, when he after carefully
reading the best of the jokes told it down the table. They
laughed. One man accidentally inhaled his cigar smoke and
spluttered, the two waiters overheard and tittered behind
their hands, one man, a bit of a raconteur himself, quite clearly
wished not to laugh, but his veins swelled dangerously in trying to keep it back, and in the end he laughed too. The joke had
succeeded; my friend smiled at the thought; he wished to say
little deprecating things to the man on his right; but the laughter did not stop and the waiters would not be silent. He waited,
and waited, wondering; the laughter went roaring on, distinctly louder now, and the waiters as loud as any. It had gone
on for three or four minutes when this frightful thought leaped
up all at once in his mind: *it was forced laughter!* How ever
could anything have induced him to tell so foolish a joke? He
saw its absurdity as in revelation; and the more he thought of
it as these people laughed at him, even the waiters too, the
more he felt that he could never lift up his head with his
brother touts again. And still the laughter went roaring and
choking on. He was very angry. There was not much use in
having a friend, he thought, if one silly joke could not be overlooked; he had fed them too. And then he felt that he had no
friends at all, and his anger faded away, and a great unhappi-
ness came down on him, and he got quietly up and slunk from
the room and slipped away from the club. Poor man, he
scarcely had the heart next morning even to glance at the
papers, but you did not need to glance at them, big type was
bandied about that day as though it were common type, the
words of the headlines stared at you; and the headlines said:
Twenty-two Dead Men at a Club.

Yes, he saw it then: the laughter had not stopped, some had
probably burst blood-vessels, some must have choked, some
succumbed to nausea, heart-failure must have mercifully
taken some, and they were his friends after all, and none had
escaped, not even the waiters. It was that infernal joke.

He thought out swiftly, and remembers clear as a nightmare
the drive to Victoria Station, the boat-train to Dover and going
disguised to the boat: and on the boat pleasantly smiling,
almost obsequious, two constables that wished to speak for a
moment with Mr. Watkyn-Jones. That was his name.

In a third-class carriage with handcuffs on his wrists, with

forced conversation when any, he returned between his captors
to Victoria to be tried for murder at the High Court of Bow.

At the trial he was defended by a young barrister of considerable ability who had gone into the Cabinet in order to enhance
his forensic reputation. And he was ably defended. It is no exag-
geration to say that the speech for the defence showed it to be
usual, even natural and right, to give a dinner to twenty men
and to slip away without ever saying a word, leaving all, with
the waiters, dead. That was the impression left in the minds of
the jury. And Mr. Watkyn-Jones felt himself practically free,
with all the advantages of his awful experience, and his two
jokes intact. But lawyers are still experimenting with the new
act which allows a prisoner to give evidence. They do not like to
make no use of it for fear they may be thought not to know of the
act, and a lawyer who is not in touch with the very latest laws
is soon regarded as not being up to date, and he may drop as
much as £50,000 a year in fees. And therefore though it always
hangs their clients they hardly like to neglect it.

Mr. Watkyn-Jones was put in the witness-box. There he told
the simple truth, and a very poor affair it seemed after the
impassioned and beautiful things that were uttered by the
counsel for the defence. Men and women had wept when they
heard that. They did not weep when they heard Watkyn-Jones.
Some tittered. It no longer seemed a right and natural thing to
leave one's guests all dead and to fly the country. Where was
Justice, they asked, if anyone could do that? And when his
story was told the judge rather happily asked if he could make
him die of laughter too. And what was the joke? For in so grave
a place as a Court of Justice no fatal effects need be feared.
And hesitatingly the prisoner pulled from his pocket the three
slips of paper: and perceived for the first time that the one on
which the first and best joke had been written had become
quite blank. Yet he could remember it, and only too clearly.
And he told it from memory to the Court.

"An Irishman once on being asked by his master to buy a
morning paper said in his usual witty way, 'Arrah and begor-
rah and I will be after wishing you the top of the morning.'"

No joke sounds quite so good the second time it is told, it seems
to lose something of its essence, but Watkyn-Jones was not prepared for the awful stillness with which this one was received;
nobody smiled; and it had killed twenty-two men. The joke was
bad, devilish bad; counsel for the defence was frowning, and an
usher was looking in a little bag for something the judge wanted.

And at this moment, as though from far away, without his wishing it, there entered the prisoner's head, and shone there and would not go, this old bad proverb: "As well be hung for a sheep as for a lamb." The jury seemed to be just about to retire. "I have another joke," said Watkyn-Jones, and then and there he read from the second slip of paper. He watched the paper curiously to see if it would go blank, occupying his mind with so slight a thing as men in dire distress very often do, and the words were almost immediately expunged, swept swiftly as if by a hand, and he saw the paper before him as blank as the first. And they were laughing this time, judge, jury, counsel for the prosecution, audience and all, and the grim men that watched him upon either side. There was no mistake about this joke.

He did not stay to see the end, and walked out with his eyes fixed on the ground, unable to bear a glance to the right or left. And since then he has wandered, avoiding ports and roaming lonely places. Two years have known him on the Highland roads, often hungry, always friendless, always changing his district, wandering lonely on with his deadly joke.

Sometimes for a moment he will enter inns, driven by cold and hunger, and hear men in the evening telling jokes, and even challenging him; but he sits desolate and silent, lest his only weapon should escape from him and his last joke spread mourning in a hundred cots. His beard has grown and turned grey and is mixed with moss and weeds, so that no one, I think, not even the police, would recognise him now for that dapper tout that sold the *Briton Dictionary of Electricity* in such a different land.

He paused, his story told, and then his lip quivered as though he would say no more, and I believe he intended then and there to yield up his deadly joke on that Highland road and to go forth then with his three blank slips of paper, perhaps to a felon's cell, with one more murder added to his crimes, but harmless at last to man. I therefore hurried on, and only heard him mumbling sadly behind me, standing bowed and broken, all alone in the twilight, perhaps telling over and over even then the last infernal joke.

A CATALOG OF SELECTED
DOVER BOOKS
IN ALL FIELDS OF INTEREST

A CATALOG OF SELECTED DOVER
BOOKS IN ALL FIELDS OF INTEREST

CONCERNING THE SPIRITUAL IN ART, Wassily Kandinsky. Pioneering work by father of abstract art. Thoughts on color theory, nature of art. Analysis of earlier masters. 12 illustrations. 80pp. of text. 5⅜ x 8½. 23411-8

ANIMALS: 1,419 Copyright-Free Illustrations of Mammals, Birds, Fish, Insects, etc., Jim Harter (ed.). Clear wood engravings present, in extremely lifelike poses, over 1,000 species of animals. One of the most extensive pictorial sourcebooks of its kind. Captions. Index. 284pp. 9 x 12. 23766-4

CELTIC ART: The Methods of Construction, George Bain. Simple geometric techniques for making Celtic interlacements, spirals, Kells-type initials, animals, humans, etc. Over 500 illustrations. 160pp. 9 x 12. (Available in U.S. only.) 22923-8

AN ATLAS OF ANATOMY FOR ARTISTS, Fritz Schider. Most thorough reference work on art anatomy in the world. Hundreds of illustrations, including selections from works by Vesalius, Leonardo, Goya, Ingres, Michelangelo, others. 593 illustrations. 192pp. 7⅛ x 10¼. 20241-0

CELTIC HAND STROKE-BY-STROKE (Irish Half-Uncial from "The Book of Kells"): An Arthur Baker Calligraphy Manual, Arthur Baker. Complete guide to creating each letter of the alphabet in distinctive Celtic manner. Covers hand position, strokes, pens, inks, paper, more. Illustrated. 48pp. 8¼ x 11. 24336-2

EASY ORIGAMI, John Montroll. Charming collection of 32 projects (hat, cup, pelican, piano, swan, many more) specially designed for the novice origami hobbyist. Clearly illustrated easy-to-follow instructions insure that even beginning papercrafters will achieve successful results. 48pp. 8¼ x 11. 27298-2

THE COMPLETE BOOK OF BIRDHOUSE CONSTRUCTION FOR WOODWORKERS, Scott D. Campbell. Detailed instructions, illustrations, tables. Also data on bird habitat and instinct patterns. Bibliography. 3 tables. 63 illustrations in 15 figures. 48pp. 5¼ x 8½. 24407-5

BLOOMINGDALE'S ILLUSTRATED 1886 CATALOG: Fashions, Dry Goods and Housewares, Bloomingdale Brothers. Famed merchants' extremely rare catalog depicting about 1,700 products: clothing, housewares, firearms, dry goods, jewelry, more. Invaluable for dating, identifying vintage items. Also, copyright-free graphics for artists, designers. Co-published with Henry Ford Museum & Greenfield Village. 160pp. 8¼ x 11. 25780-0

HISTORIC COSTUME IN PICTURES, Braun & Schneider. Over 1,450 costumed figures in clearly detailed engravings—from dawn of civilization to end of 19th century. Captions. Many folk costumes. 256pp. 8⅜ x 11¾. 23150-X

STICKLEY CRAFTSMAN FURNITURE CATALOGS, Gustav Stickley and L. & J. G. Stickley. Beautiful, functional furniture in two authentic catalogs from 1910. 594 illustrations, including 277 photos, show settles, rockers, armchairs, reclining chairs, bookcases, desks, tables. 183pp. 6½ x 9¼. 23838-5

AMERICAN LOCOMOTIVES IN HISTORIC PHOTOGRAPHS: 1858 to 1949, Ron Ziel (ed.). A rare collection of 126 meticulously detailed official photographs, called "builder portraits," of American locomotives that majestically chronicle the rise of steam locomotive power in America. Introduction. Detailed captions. xi+ 129pp. 9 x 12. 27393-8

AMERICA'S LIGHTHOUSES: An Illustrated History, Francis Ross Holland, Jr. Delightfully written, profusely illustrated fact-filled survey of over 200 American lighthouses since 1716. History, anecdotes, technological advances, more. 240pp. 8 x 10¾. 25576-X

TOWARDS A NEW ARCHITECTURE, Le Corbusier. Pioneering manifesto by founder of "International School." Technical and aesthetic theories, views of industry, economics, relation of form to function, "mass-production split" and much more. Profusely illustrated. 320pp. 6⅛ x 9¼. (Available in U.S. only.) 25023-7

HOW THE OTHER HALF LIVES, Jacob Riis. Famous journalistic record, exposing poverty and degradation of New York slums around 1900, by major social reformer. 100 striking and influential photographs. 233pp. 10 x 7⅞. 22012-5

FRUIT KEY AND TWIG KEY TO TREES AND SHRUBS, William M. Harlow. One of the handiest and most widely used identification aids. Fruit key covers 120 deciduous and evergreen species; twig key 160 deciduous species. Easily used. Over 300 photographs. 126pp. 5⅜ x 8½. 20511-8

COMMON BIRD SONGS, Dr. Donald J. Borror. Songs of 60 most common U.S. birds: robins, sparrows, cardinals, bluejays, finches, more–arranged in order of increasing complexity. Up to 9 variations of songs of each species.
Cassette and manual 99911-4

ORCHIDS AS HOUSE PLANTS, Rebecca Tyson Northen. Grow cattleyas and many other kinds of orchids–in a window, in a case, or under artificial light. 63 illustrations. 148pp. 5⅜ x 8½. 23261-1

MONSTER MAZES, Dave Phillips. Masterful mazes at four levels of difficulty. Avoid deadly perils and evil creatures to find magical treasures. Solutions for all 32 exciting illustrated puzzles. 48pp. 8¼ x 11. 26005-4

MOZART'S DON GIOVANNI (DOVER OPERA LIBRETTO SERIES), Wolfgang Amadeus Mozart. Introduced and translated by Ellen H. Bleiler. Standard Italian libretto, with complete English translation. Convenient and thoroughly portable–an ideal companion for reading along with a recording or the performance itself. Introduction. List of characters. Plot summary. 121pp. 5¼ x 8½. 24944-1

TECHNICAL MANUAL AND DICTIONARY OF CLASSICAL BALLET, Gail Grant. Defines, explains, comments on steps, movements, poses and concepts. 15-page pictorial section. Basic book for student, viewer. 127pp. 5⅜ x 8½. 21843-0

CATALOG OF DOVER BOOKS

ANATOMY: A Complete Guide for Artists, Joseph Sheppard. A master of figure drawing shows artists how to render human anatomy convincingly. Over 460 illustrations. 224pp. 8⅜ x 11¼. 27279-6

MEDIEVAL CALLIGRAPHY: Its History and Technique, Marc Drogin. Spirited history, comprehensive instruction manual covers 13 styles (ca. 4th century through 15th). Excellent photographs; directions for duplicating medieval techniques with modern tools. 224pp. 8⅜ x 11¼. 26142-5

DRIED FLOWERS: How to Prepare Them, Sarah Whitlock and Martha Rankin. Complete instructions on how to use silica gel, meal and borax, perlite aggregate, sand and borax, glycerine and water to create attractive permanent flower arrangements. 12 illustrations. 32pp. 5⅜ x 8½. 21802-3

EASY-TO-MAKE BIRD FEEDERS FOR WOODWORKERS, Scott D. Campbell. Detailed, simple-to-use guide for designing, constructing, caring for and using feeders. Text, illustrations for 12 classic and contemporary designs. 96pp. 5⅜ x 8½. 25847-5

SCOTTISH WONDER TALES FROM MYTH AND LEGEND, Donald A. Mackenzie. 16 lively tales tell of giants rumbling down mountainsides, of a magic wand that turns stone pillars into warriors, of gods and goddesses, evil hags, powerful forces and more. 240pp. 5⅜ x 8½. 29677-6

THE HISTORY OF UNDERCLOTHES, C. Willett Cunnington and Phyllis Cunnington. Fascinating, well-documented survey covering six centuries of English undergarments, enhanced with over 100 illustrations: 12th-century laced-up bodice, footed long drawers (1795), 19th-century bustles, 19th-century corsets for men, Victorian "bust improvers," much more. 272pp. 5⅝ x 8¼. 27124-2

ARTS AND CRAFTS FURNITURE: The Complete Brooks Catalog of 1912, Brooks Manufacturing Co. Photos and detailed descriptions of more than 150 now very collectible furniture designs from the Arts and Crafts movement depict davenports, settees, buffets, desks, tables, chairs, bedsteads, dressers and more, all built of solid, quarter-sawed oak. Invaluable for students and enthusiasts of antiques, Americana and the decorative arts. 80pp. 6½ x 9¼. 27471-3

WILBUR AND ORVILLE: A Biography of the Wright Brothers, Fred Howard. Definitive, crisply written study tells the full story of the brothers' lives and work. A vividly written biography, unparalleled in scope and color, that also captures the spirit of an extraordinary era. 560pp. 6⅛ x 9¼. 40297-5

THE ARTS OF THE SAILOR: Knotting, Splicing and Ropework, Hervey Garrett Smith. Indispensable shipboard reference covers tools, basic knots and useful hitches; handsewing and canvas work, more. Over 100 illustrations. Delightful reading for sea lovers. 256pp. 5⅜ x 8½. 26440-8

FRANK LLOYD WRIGHT'S FALLINGWATER: The House and Its History, Second, Revised Edition, Donald Hoffmann. A total revision–both in text and illustrations–of the standard document on Fallingwater, the boldest, most personal architectural statement of Wright's mature years, updated with valuable new material from the recently opened Frank Lloyd Wright Archives. "Fascinating"–*The New York Times.* 116 illustrations. 128pp. 9¼ x 10¾. 27430-6

THE WIT AND HUMOR OF OSCAR WILDE, Alvin Redman (ed.). More than 1,000 ripostes, paradoxes, wisecracks: Work is the curse of the drinking classes; I can resist everything except temptation; etc. 258pp. 5⅜ x 8½.   20602-5

SHAKESPEARE LEXICON AND QUOTATION DICTIONARY, Alexander Schmidt. Full definitions, locations, shades of meaning in every word in plays and poems. More than 50,000 exact quotations. 1,485pp. 6½ x 9¼. 2-vol. set.
Vol. 1: 22726-X
Vol. 2: 22727-8

SELECTED POEMS, Emily Dickinson. Over 100 best-known, best-loved poems by one of America's foremost poets, reprinted from authoritative early editions. No comparable edition at this price. Index of first lines. 64pp. 5³⁄₁₆ x 8¼.   26466-1

THE INSIDIOUS DR. FU-MANCHU, Sax Rohmer. The first of the popular mystery series introduces a pair of English detectives to their archnemesis, the diabolical Dr. Fu-Manchu. Flavorful atmosphere, fast-paced action, and colorful characters enliven this classic of the genre. 208pp. 5³⁄₁₆ x 8¼.   29898-1

THE MALLEUS MALEFICARUM OF KRAMER AND SPRENGER, translated by Montague Summers. Full text of most important witchhunter's "bible," used by both Catholics and Protestants. 278pp. 6⅝ x 10.   22802-9

SPANISH STORIES/CUENTOS ESPAÑOLES: A Dual-Language Book, Angel Flores (ed.). Unique format offers 13 great stories in Spanish by Cervantes, Borges, others. Faithful English translations on facing pages. 352pp. 5⅜ x 8½.   25399-6

GARDEN CITY, LONG ISLAND, IN EARLY PHOTOGRAPHS, 1869–1919, Mildred H. Smith. Handsome treasury of 118 vintage pictures, accompanied by carefully researched captions, document the Garden City Hotel fire (1899), the Vanderbilt Cup Race (1908), the first airmail flight departing from the Nassau Boulevard Aerodrome (1911), and much more. 96pp. 8⅞ x 11¾.   40669-5

OLD QUEENS, N.Y., IN EARLY PHOTOGRAPHS, Vincent F. Seyfried and William Asadorian. Over 160 rare photographs of Maspeth, Jamaica, Jackson Heights, and other areas. Vintage views of DeWitt Clinton mansion, 1939 World's Fair and more. Captions. 192pp. 8⅞ x 11.   26358-4

CAPTURED BY THE INDIANS: 15 Firsthand Accounts, 1750-1870, Frederick Drimmer. Astounding true historical accounts of grisly torture, bloody conflicts, relentless pursuits, miraculous escapes and more, by people who lived to tell the tale. 384pp. 5⅜ x 8½.   24901-8

THE WORLD'S GREAT SPEECHES (Fourth Enlarged Edition), Lewis Copeland, Lawrence W. Lamm, and Stephen J. McKenna. Nearly 300 speeches provide public speakers with a wealth of updated quotes and inspiration–from Pericles' funeral oration and William Jennings Bryan's "Cross of Gold Speech" to Malcolm X's powerful words on the Black Revolution and Earl of Spenser's tribute to his sister, Diana, Princess of Wales. 944pp. 5⅜ x 8⅜.   40903-1

THE BOOK OF THE SWORD, Sir Richard F. Burton. Great Victorian scholar/adventurer's eloquent, erudite history of the "queen of weapons"–from prehistory to early Roman Empire. Evolution and development of early swords, variations (sabre, broadsword, cutlass, scimitar, etc.), much more. 336pp. 6⅛ x 9¼.
25434-8

AUTOBIOGRAPHY: The Story of My Experiments with Truth, Mohandas K. Gandhi. Boyhood, legal studies, purification, the growth of the Satyagraha (nonviolent protest) movement. Critical, inspiring work of the man responsible for the freedom of India. 480pp. 5⅜ x 8½. (Available in U.S. only.) 24593-4

CELTIC MYTHS AND LEGENDS, T. W. Rolleston. Masterful retelling of Irish and Welsh stories and tales. Cuchulain, King Arthur, Deirdre, the Grail, many more. First paperback edition. 58 full-page illustrations. 512pp. 5⅜ x 8½. 26507-2

THE PRINCIPLES OF PSYCHOLOGY, William James. Famous long course complete, unabridged. Stream of thought, time perception, memory, experimental methods; great work decades ahead of its time. 94 figures. 1,391pp. 5⅜ x 8½. 2-vol. set.
Vol. I: 20381-6 Vol. II: 20382-4

THE WORLD AS WILL AND REPRESENTATION, Arthur Schopenhauer. Definitive English translation of Schopenhauer's life work, correcting more than 1,000 errors, omissions in earlier translations. Translated by E. F. J. Payne. Total of 1,269pp. 5⅜ x 8½. 2-vol. set. Vol. 1: 21761-2 Vol. 2: 21762-0

MAGIC AND MYSTERY IN TIBET, Madame Alexandra David-Neel. Experiences among lamas, magicians, sages, sorcerers, Bonpa wizards. A true psychic discovery. 32 illustrations. 321pp. 5⅜ x 8½. (Available in U.S. only.) 22682-4

THE EGYPTIAN BOOK OF THE DEAD, E. A. Wallis Budge. Complete reproduction of Ani's papyrus, finest ever found. Full hieroglyphic text, interlinear transliteration, word-for-word translation, smooth translation. 533pp. 6½ x 9¼. 21866-X

MATHEMATICS FOR THE NONMATHEMATICIAN, Morris Kline. Detailed, college-level treatment of mathematics in cultural and historical context, with numerous exercises. Recommended Reading Lists. Tables. Numerous figures. 641pp. 5⅜ x 8½. 24823-2

PROBABILISTIC METHODS IN THE THEORY OF STRUCTURES, Isaac Elishakoff. Well-written introduction covers the elements of the theory of probability from two or more random variables, the reliability of such multivariable structures, the theory of random function, Monte Carlo methods of treating problems incapable of exact solution, and more. Examples. 502pp. 5⅜ x 8½. 40691-1

THE RIME OF THE ANCIENT MARINER, Gustave Doré, S. T. Coleridge. Doré's finest work; 34 plates capture moods, subtleties of poem. Flawless full-size reproductions printed on facing pages with authoritative text of poem. "Beautiful. Simply beautiful."–*Publisher's Weekly*. 77pp. 9¼ x 12. 22305-1

NORTH AMERICAN INDIAN DESIGNS FOR ARTISTS AND CRAFTSPEOPLE, Eva Wilson. Over 360 authentic copyright-free designs adapted from Navajo blankets, Hopi pottery, Sioux buffalo hides, more. Geometrics, symbolic figures, plant and animal motifs, etc. 128pp. 8⅜ x 11. (Not for sale in the United Kingdom.) 25341-4

SCULPTURE: Principles and Practice, Louis Slobodkin. Step-by-step approach to clay, plaster, metals, stone; classical and modern. 253 drawings, photos. 255pp. 8⅛ x 11. 22960-2

THE INFLUENCE OF SEA POWER UPON HISTORY, 1660–1783, A. T. Mahan. Influential classic of naval history and tactics still used as text in war colleges. First paperback edition. 4 maps. 24 battle plans. 640pp. 5⅜ x 8½. 25509-3

THE STORY OF THE TITANIC AS TOLD BY ITS SURVIVORS, Jack Winocour
(ed.). What it was really like. Panic, despair, shocking inefficiency, and a little hero-
ism. More thrilling than any fictional account. 26 illustrations. 320pp. 5⅜ x 8½.
                                                                          20610-6

FAIRY AND FOLK TALES OF THE IRISH PEASANTRY, William Butler Yeats
(ed.). Treasury of 64 tales from the twilight world of Celtic myth and legend: "The
Soul Cages," "The Kildare Pooka," "King O'Toole and his Goose," many more.
Introduction and Notes by W. B. Yeats. 352pp. 5⅜ x 8½.   26941-8

BUDDHIST MAHAYANA TEXTS, E. B. Cowell and others (eds.). Superb, accu-
rate translations of basic documents in Mahayana Buddhism, highly important in history of religions. The Buddha-karita of Asvaghosha, Larger Sukhavativyuha, more.
448pp. 5⅜ x 8½.   25552-2

ONE TWO THREE . . . INFINITY: Facts and Speculations of Science, George
Gamow. Great physicist's fascinating, readable overview of contemporary science:
number theory, relativity, fourth dimension, entropy, genes, atomic structure, much
more. 128 illustrations. Index. 352pp. 5⅜ x 8½.   25664-2

EXPERIMENTATION AND MEASUREMENT, W. J. Youden. Introductory man-
ual explains laws of measurement in simple terms and offers tips for achieving accu-
racy and minimizing errors. Mathematics of measurement, use of instruments, experimenting with machines. 1994 edition. Foreword. Preface. Introduction. Epilogue.
Selected Readings. Glossary. Index. Tables and figures. 128pp. 5⅜ x 8½.   40451-X

DALÍ ON MODERN ART: The Cuckolds of Antiquated Modern Art, Salvador Dalí.
Influential painter skewers modern art and its practitioners. Outrageous evaluations of
Picasso, Cézanne, Turner, more. 15 renderings of paintings discussed. 44 calligraphic
decorations by Dalí. 96pp. 5⅜ x 8½. (Available in U.S. only.)   29220-7

ANTIQUE PLAYING CARDS: A Pictorial History, Henry René D'Allemagne.
Over 900 elaborate, decorative images from rare playing cards (14th–20th centuries):
Bacchus, death, dancing dogs, hunting scenes, royal coats of arms, players cheating,
much more. 96pp. 9¼ x 12¼.   29265-7

MAKING FURNITURE MASTERPIECES: 30 Projects with Measured Drawings,
Franklin H. Gottshall. Step-by-step instructions, illustrations for constructing hand-
some, useful pieces, among them a Sheraton desk, Chippendale chair, Spanish desk,
Queen Anne table and a William and Mary dressing mirror. 224pp. 8⅛ x 11¼.
                                                                          29338-6

THE FOSSIL BOOK: A Record of Prehistoric Life, Patricia V. Rich et al. Profusely
illustrated definitive guide covers everything from single-celled organisms and
dinosaurs to birds and mammals and the interplay between climate and man. Over
1,500 illustrations. 760pp. 7½ x 10⅛.   29371-8

Paperbound unless otherwise indicated. Available at your book dealer, online at
www.doverpublications.com, or by writing to Dept. GI, Dover Publications, Inc., 31 East 2nd
Street, Mineola, NY 11501. For current price information or for free catalogues (please indicate
field of interest), write to Dover Publications or log on to **www.doverpublications.com** and see
every Dover book in print. Dover publishes more than 500 books each year on science, elementary
and advanced mathematics, biology, music, art, literary history, social sciences, and other areas.